·大学生读书计划·
University Reader

英汉对照·中国文学宝库·古代文学系列
English-Chinese·Gems of Chinese Literature·Classical

古代寓言选
Selected Fables from Old Cathay

偬 仕 编
Compiled by Zong Shi

中国文学出版社
Chinese Literature Press
外语教学与研究出版社
Foreign Language Teaching and Research Press

图书在版编目(CIP)数据

古代寓言选:英汉对照/偬仕编.—北京:中国文学出版社:
外语教学与研究出版社,1999.8
(中国文学宝库·古代文学系列)
ISBN 7-5071-0531-8

Ⅰ.古… Ⅱ.偬… Ⅲ.寓言-中国-古代-对照读物-英、汉 Ⅳ.
H319.4:I

中国版本图书馆 CIP 数据核字(1999)第 23453 号

中文责编:吴善祥 沈洁莹
英文责编:殷 雯

英汉对照 中国文学宝库·古代文学系列
古代寓言选
偬 仕编

中国文学出版社
(北京百万庄路24号) 出版发行
外语教学与研究出版社
(北京西三环北路19号)

北京市鑫鑫印刷厂印刷
新华书店总店北京发行所经销

开本 850×1168 1/32 6.625 印张
1999年8月第1版 1999年8月第1次印刷
字数:95 千 印数:1—5000 册

ISBN 7-5071-0531-8/I·497
定价:7.90 元

总编辑 杨宪益 戴乃迭

总策划 野 莽 蔡剑峰

编委会(以姓氏笔划为序)

吕 华

李朋义

赵文炎

凌 原

野 莽

蔡剑峰

目 录
CONTENTS

大学生读书计划 ……………………… 编 者（Ⅰ）
　　——中国文学宝库出版呼吁
How the Fool Moved Mountains …………… (2)
愚公移山 ……………………………………… (3)
The Lord Who Loved Dragons …………… (6)
叶公好龙 ……………………………………… (7)
The Rats in the Altar ……………………… (8)
社鼠 …………………………………………… (9)
The Chicken Thief ………………………… (10)
攘鸡 …………………………………………… (11)
Waiting for a Hare to Turn up …………… (12)
守株待兔 ……………………………………… (13)
The Fox Who Profited by the Tiger's Might ……… (14)
狐假虎威 ……………………………………… (15)
The Snipe and the Mussel ………………… (16)
鹬蚌相争 ……………………………………… (17)
The Wolf of Zhongshan …………………… (18)
中山狼传 ……………………………………… (19)
Entering the City Gate with a Long Pole ……… (38)
截竿入城 ……………………………………… (39)
Punishing the Horse ……………………… (40)
取道杀马 ……………………………………… (41)

1

目录

Why Zeng Shen Killed the Pig ……………………（42）
曾子杀猪 …………………………………………（43）
The Dog Who Soured Wine ……………………（44）
狗猛酒酸 …………………………………………（45）
Tht Use of Parables ……………………………（46）
惠子善譬 …………………………………………（47）
The Cicada, the Praying Mantis and the Sparrow …（48）
螳螂捕蝉 …………………………………………（49）
The Fur and the Hide …………………………（50）
反裘负刍 …………………………………………（51）
The Man Who Lost His Jacket ………………（52）
澄子亡缁衣 ………………………………………（53）
The Owl Moves House …………………………（54）
枭将东徙 …………………………………………（55）
Buying a Pair of Shoes ………………………（56）
郑人买履 …………………………………………（57）
Marking the Boat to Locate the Sword ………（58）
刻舟求剑 …………………………………………（59）
Too Many Paths …………………………………（60）
多歧亡羊 …………………………………………（61）
Presenting Doves ………………………………（62）
献鸠 ………………………………………………（63）
Felling the Plane Tree …………………………（64）
枯梧不祥 …………………………………………（65）
The Man Who Saw Nobody ……………………（66）
攫金 ………………………………………………（67）
The Ointment for Chapped Hands ……………（68）

目录

不龟手之药 …………………………………（69）
The Bird Killed by Kindness ……………………（70）
鲁侯养鸟 …………………………………（71）
Learning the Wrong Thing ……………………（72）
丑女效颦 …………………………………（73）
The Frog in the Well ……………………………（74）
埳井之蛙 …………………………………（75）
The Carp in the Dry Rut ………………………（76）
辙中有鲋 …………………………………（77）
How Two Shepherd Boys Lost Their Sheep ……（78）
臧谷亡羊 …………………………………（79）
Three Chestnuts or Four ………………………（80）
狙公赋芋 …………………………………（81）
The Prince and His Bow ………………………（82）
宣王好射 …………………………………（83）
Learning to Play Draughts ……………………（84）
学弈 ………………………………………（85）
Helping Young Shoots to Grow ………………（86）
揠苗助长 …………………………………（87）
The Man Who Was Afraid of Ghosts …………（88）
涓蜀梁 ……………………………………（89）
The Man Who Was Found in the Well …………（90）
穿井得一人 ………………………………（91）
The Son of a Good Swimmer …………………（92）
其父善游 …………………………………（93）
Stealing the Bell …………………………………（94）
掩耳盗钟 …………………………………（95）

3

目录

Painting Ghosts ………………………………………… (96)
说画 ……………………………………………………… (97)
The Crumbling Wall …………………………………… (98)
宋有富人 ………………………………………………… (99)
Ivory Chopsticks ………………………………………… (100)
纣为象箸 ………………………………………………… (101)
The Man Who Pretended He Could Play Reed Pipes … (102)
滥竽充数 ………………………………………………… (103)
The Man Who Sold Spears and Shields ……………… (104)
矛盾 ……………………………………………………… (105)
A Recipe for Immortality ……………………………… (106)
燕王学道 ………………………………………………… (107)
How Two Water Snakes Moved House ……………… (108)
涸泽之蛇 ………………………………………………… (109)
Selling the Casket Without the Pearls ………………… (110)
买椟还珠 ………………………………………………… (111)
The Rumour About Zeng Shen ………………………… (112)
曾母投杼 ………………………………………………… (113)
The Wrong Direction …………………………………… (114)
南辕北辙 ………………………………………………… (115)
Drawing a Snake with Legs …………………………… (116)
画蛇添足 ………………………………………………… (117)
Buying a Good Horse …………………………………… (118)
千金买首 ………………………………………………… (119)
Who Deserved the Place of Honour …………………… (120)
曲突徙薪 ………………………………………………… (121)
Playing the Harp to an Ox …………………………… (122)

4

对牛弹琴 …… (123)
Lamenting a Mother's Death …… (124)
哭母不哀 …… (125)
A Scholar Buys a Donkey …… (126)
博士买驴 …… (127)
The Man Who Liked Money Better Than Life …… (128)
溺者之死货 …… (129)
The Donkey of Guizhou …… (130)
黔之驴 …… (131)
The Silly Fawn …… (132)
临江之麋 …… (133)
Ancient Books for Ancient Bronze …… (134)
古书换古器 …… (135)
The Boat-Owner's Bright Idea …… (136)
可折半直 …… (137)
What Does the Sun Look Like? …… (138)
日喻 …… (139)
The Fighting Oxen …… (140)
戴嵩画牛 …… (141)
Treating Hunchbacks …… (142)
驼医 …… (143)
The Dream …… (144)
狡生梦金 …… (145)
Nothing to Do with Me …… (148)
任事 …… (149)
Laugh with Others …… (150)
众笑亦笑 …… (151)

目录

Fine Tung Wood	(152)
良桐	(153)
Drought Assails the East Capital	(154)
东都大旱	(155)
Saving a Tiger	(156)
道士救虎	(157)
The Malicious Intent of Ziqiao	(158)
西郭子侨	(159)
The Musk Deer and the Tiger	(160)
麋虎	(161)
Wisdom and Strength	(162)
智力	(163)
Beekeepers	(164)
灵丘丈人养蜂	(165)
A Merchant	(168)
济阴商人	(169)
The Nine-Headed Bird	(170)
九头鸟争食	(171)
Jue Shu's Three Regrets	(172)
蹶叔三悔	(173)
An Impetuous Person	(176)
躁人	(177)
Stealing Dregs	(178)
鲁人窃糟	(179)
Preemptive Surgery	(180)
刳马肝	(181)
A Bull Wearing a Kerchief	(182)

富翁戴巾	(183)
Better to Be Blind	(184)
宁为盲人	(185)
Parents for Sale	(186)
卖双亲	(187)
Evading a Debt	(188)
躲债	(189)
Retractility	(190)
答令尊	(191)
To Readers of the English Translations of Classical Chinese Prose and Poetry ……………… Revisor	(192)
关于中国古典文学作品英译文的说明 ……… 校译者	(196)

大学生读书计划
——中国文学宝库出版呼吁

在即将开机印刷这第一批50本名为中国文学宝库的英汉对照读本时,我们的心情竟然忧多于喜。因为我们只能以保守的5000册印数,去面对全国400万在校大学生。

虽然我们并非市场经济的局外者,若仅为印数(销售量)计,大可奋起而去生产诸如TOFEL应试指南,或者英语四六级模拟试题集一类的教辅图书,但我们还是决定宁可冒着债台高筑的风险,也有责任对大学生同胞发出一声亲切的呼唤:请亲近我们的中国文学。

身为向世界译介中国文学和向国内出版外语读物的,具有双重责任的出版社,我们得知目前大学生往往仅注重外语的学习而偏废了母语的提高,以及忽视了中国文学的阅读,放弃了人文知识的训练。有统计表明,某理工院校57%的同学不曾读过《红楼梦》等四大名著,以致校园内外流行着"样子像研究生,说话像大学生,作文像中学生,写字像小学生"的幽默。还有一副这样的对联,说大学生的文章是"无错不成文,病句错句破残句,句句不堪入目;有误方为篇,别字错字自造字,字字触目惊心",横批"斯文扫地"。作为未来社会中坚和整个社会发展关键力量的大学生,这种"文弃"现象的流行,势必导致一场人文精神危机的爆发。对照以科学与人文精神追求为主题的五四新文化运动,八十年的历程告诉我们,以上提醒绝非危言耸听。

我们已经迈入知识经济时代,在追求科学知识的同时,创新精神已成为关键;而创新的源泉其实有赖于多学科多领域知识的交融,依靠的是新型的复合型人才,所以,文学对于新一代的大学生来说绝非装点,而是沟通自然科学与人文科学的桥梁,使我们在汲取知识的同时更能获得智慧,于创造物质的同时还进一步丰富和完善着精神;无怪乎爱因斯坦认为自己受影响最大的竟是陀思妥耶夫斯基。由此证明,一个真正的科学家应该拥有丰富的文学和文化知识以及完整的人格。十年前,七十五位诺贝尔奖得主聚会巴黎,当时他们所发表的宣言开篇就是,"如果人类要在21世纪生存下去,必须回首2500年去吸收孔子的智慧。"确实,十年的时间让我们有目共睹,现代经济科技的飞速发展何尝不是一柄双刃的剑?只有文化的力量才能抵消随之而来的负面后果。可见,知识的获取与技能的训练对于大学生来说固然重要,但文化与修养却尤需关切。正因为大学生代表着社会先知先觉的知识力量,置身当前的文化现实,就应有一分责任感与使命感,力求对知识技能以外许多带有根本性质的精神追求形成明确的意识,从而具备一种对生命意义进行探索与追问的精神,一种以人文精神为背景的生存勇气和人格力量。那么,能够引导我们探索前行的一盏明灯,不就是闪烁着理想光芒的不朽的文学名著吗?

一个人乃至一个民族,从其对文学的亲疏态度,可以衡量出其文化素质的程度。文学应是从人类文化中升华出的理想的结晶,她"使人的心灵变得高尚,使人的勇气、荣誉感、希望、尊严、同情心、怜悯心和牺牲精神复活起来"(威廉·福克纳);无疑,只有文学才能从更高的层次上提升人的文化素质和整体素质,充实人的内心世界,焕发人的精神风貌,带给人们真善美。而亲近文学,特别是热爱祖国灿烂的文学以及文化,正是当代中国大学生加强文化修养,弘扬人文精神的有力脚步。

"越是民族的,就越是世界的",中国文学属于中国,也属于世界。和平是人类的共同愿望,交流与共享则是新世纪的潮流。

中国当代大学生的血液里流动着数千年的文化积淀,没有理由在让世界了解中国大学生聪明才智的同时,却无缘分享我们的骄傲——中国大学生不但能够读懂英语的莎士比亚,而且能让世界感动于中国文学的伟大。

这是我们作为出版者的理想。我们原有一个世纪礼物的构想,是同大学生一起做一个"读书计划"。这一次将中国文学的最新荟萃配设高水平的英语译文,是其中推荐给新世纪大学生的第一批读物。盼望着您——我们无数知音中的5000名先来者,给我们鼓励,也给我们意见和批评。

编者
一九九九年五月三十日

只有文学才能从更高的层次上提升人的文化素质和整体素质,充实人的内心世界,焕发人的精神风貌,带给人们真善美。而亲近文学,特别是热爱祖国灿烂的文学以及文化,正是当代中国大学生加强文化修养,弘扬人文精神的有力脚步。

How the Fool Moved Mountains

The Taihang and Wangwu Mountains are seven hundred *li* around and hundreds of thousands of feet high.

The Fool who lived north or the mountains was nearly ninety. His house faced these mountains, and finding it most inconvenient to have his entrance blocked by them so that he had to go round each time he went out or came back, he summoned his family to discuss the matter.

"Suppose we work together to level the moutains?" he suggested. "Then we can open a road through Yunan to Hanying. How about it?"

They all agreed.

Only his wife was dubious and said, "You haven't the strength to raze a small hill like Kuifu. How can you move the Taihang and Wangwu Mountains? Besides, where will you dump all the earth and rocks?"

They answered, "We'll dump them in the sea."

愚公移山

太形、王屋二山①,方七百里,高万仞。本在冀州之南②,河阳之北③。

北方愚公者,年且九十④,面山而居。惩山北之塞⑤,出入之迂也⑥,聚室而谋,曰:"吾与汝毕力平险,指通豫南⑦,达于汉阴⑧,可乎?"杂然相许⑨。

其妻献疑曰⑩:"以君之力,曾不能损魁父⑪之丘,如太形、王屋何?且焉置土石⑫?"杂曰:"投诸渤海之尾⑬,隐土之北⑭。"

---

① 太形,即"太行",主峰在今山西省晋城县南。王屋山在今阳城县西南,山有三重,状似房屋。
② 冀州:古九州之一,包括今河北、山西二省,及辽宁省辽河以西和河南省黄河以北地区。
③ 河阳:在今河南省孟县境内。
④ 且:将近。
⑤ 惩(chéng 成):苦。
⑥ 迂:曲折绕路。
⑦ 豫南:豫州南部。豫,今河南省简称。
⑧ 汉阴:汉水南边。古时称山之北及水之南为"阴",山之南及水之北为"阳"。
⑨ 杂然相许:纷纷表示赞成。
⑩ 献疑:提出疑问,表示为难。
⑪ 曾:与"尚"、"还"相当。魁父:小山名,在今河南省陈留县。
⑫ 焉:哪里、何。
⑬ 投诸渤海之尾:把它们扔到渤海的后面。
⑭ 隐土:传说中的地名。

英汉对照
English-Chinese
中国文学宝库
Gems of Chinese Literature
古代文学系列
Classical Literature

Then the Fool set out with his son and grandson, the three of them carrying poles. They dug up stones and earth and carried them in baskets to the tip of Bohai. A neighbour of theirs named Jingcheng left a widow with a son of seven or eight, and this boy came bounding over to help them. It took them from winter to summer to make one trip.

The Wise Man living at the river bend laughed at them and tried to stop them.

"Enough of this folly!" he cried. "How stupid you are! A man as old and weak as you won't be able to move a fraction of these mountains. How can you dispose of so much earth and rocks?"

The Fool from north of the mountains heaved a long sigh.

"How dull and dense you are," he said. "You haven't as much sense as the widow's young son. Though I die, I shall leave behind my son and my son's sons, and so on from generation to generation without end. Since the mountains can't grow any larger, why shouldn't we be able to level them?"

Then the Wise Man had nothing to say.

愚公移山

遂率子孙荷担者三夫①，叩石垦壤②，箕畚运于渤海之尾③。邻人京城氏之孀妻④，有遗男始龀⑤，跳往助之。寒暑易节⑥，始一反焉。

河曲智叟笑而止之，曰："甚矣！汝之不惠⑦。以残年余力，曾不能毁山之一毛，其如土石何？"

北山愚公长息曰："汝心之固⑧，固不可彻⑨。曾不若孀妻弱子。虽我之死，有子存焉。子又生孙，孙又生子，子又有子，子又有孙，子子孙孙，无穷匮也⑩。而山不加增，何苦而不平⑪？"

河曲智叟亡以应。

---

① 夫：人。古时对成年男子的通称。
② 叩石垦壤：指凿石挖土。
③ 箕畚(běn本)：挑土用的盛器，用竹编成。
④ 京城：复姓。孀(shuāng双)妻：寡妇。
⑤ 遗男：孤儿。始龀(chèn趁)：才换牙齿。
⑥ 易节：换季节。
⑦ 惠："同慧"，借用字。
⑧ 固：顽固。
⑨ 彻：通彻。
⑩ 穷匮(kuì溃)：穷尽、困乏。
⑪ 何苦：何患、怎么怕。

英汉对照
English-Chinese
中国文学宝库
Gems of Chinese Literature
古代文学系列
Classical Literature

The Lord Who Loved Dragons

Zigao the Lord of Ye* was so fond of dragons that he had them painted and carved all over his house.

The dragon in heaven, hearing of this, came down to thrust its head through the lord's door and put its tail through the window. At this sight, the Lord of Ye fled, frightened nearly out of his wits.

This shows that the Lord of Ye was not truly fond of dragons. He liked what looked like a dragon, not the real things.

---

* Pronounced "she" in ancient times.

叶公好龙

叶公子高好龙①,钩以写龙②,凿以写龙③,屋室雕文以写龙。

于是天龙闻而下之,窥头于牖④,施尾于堂⑤。叶公见之,弃而还走⑥,失其魂魄,五色无主⑦。

是叶公非好龙也,好夫似龙而非龙者也。

---

① 叶(旧读 shè 摄)公子高:名诸梁,字子高,为楚国贵族,封于叶(今河南省叶县),所以称叶公子高。
② 钩:指衣带钩,是衣服上的装饰品。写:这里指刻画。下同。
③ 凿:为"爵"的假借字。爵,酒杯。
④ 牖(yǒu 有):窗户。
⑤ 施(yì 意):拖。
⑥ 还走:转身而逃。
⑦ 五色无主:吓得失魂落魄、面无人色。五色,指脸色和神情。无主,失去自控力,难以自主。

英汉对照
English-Chinese
中国文学宝库
Gems of Chinese Literature
古代文学系列
Classical Literature

The Rats in the Altar

An altar is enclosed in wooden palisades and painted over; then rats move in to live in it. If men try to smoke the rats out, they risk burning the wood. If they try to drown them with water, they risk spoiling the paint.

Thus the rats cannot be destroyed on account of the altar.

社 鼠①

夫社,束木而涂之②,鼠因往托焉③。
熏之则恐烧其木④,灌之则恐败其涂⑤。此鼠所以不可得杀者,以社故也。

---

① 社鼠:土地庙中的老鼠。古人封土立社,祈福报功。被祭祀的神或祭祀的场所都称作"社"。
② 束木:树立起木板。束,捆绑。束木,《韩非子·外储说右上》作"树木"。涂:涂泥,抹泥于墙。
③ 托:寄托、寄身。
④ 熏:以火烟熏炙。
⑤ 涂:抹泥于墙,所以这里也可解作"墙"。

英汉对照
English-Chinese
中国文学宝库
Gems of Chinese Literature
古代文学系列
Classical Literature

The Chicken Thief

There was a man who used to steal a chicken from his neighbours every day.

"A superior man does not steal," someone told him.

"I'll cut down on it," he said. "I shall steal one chicken a month from now on and stop altogether next year."

Since he knew he was wrong, he ought to have stopped at once. Why wait for another year?

攘 鸡

今有人，日攘其邻之鸡者①。

或告之曰："是非君子之道。"

曰："请损之②，月攘一鸡，以待来年，然后已③。"

---

① 攘(rǎng 嚷)：窃取。
② 损：减少，减轻。
③ 已：停止。

Waiting for a Hare to Turn up

There was a peasant in the land of Song who had a tree in his field. One day a hare dashed up, knocked against the tree and fell dead with its neck broken. Then the peasant put down his hoe and waited by the tree for another hare to turn up. No more hares appeared, however, but he became the laughing-stock of the land.

守株待兔①

宋人有耕者,田中有株,兔走触株,折颈而死。因释其耒而守株②,冀复得兔③。

兔不可复得,而身为宋国笑。

---

① 株:树桩子。在土中称根,露在地面上的称株。
② 释:放下。耒(lěi 垒):古代农具,类似犁杖。
③ 冀(jì 记):希望。

The Fox Who Profited by the Tiger's Might

A tiger, looking for some prey, caught a fox.

"Don't you dare eat me!" said the fox. "The Emperor of Heaven has appointed me king of the beasts. If you eat me, you will be disobeying his orders. If you don't believe me, let me walk ahead while you follow close behind. You'll see whether the other beasts run away at the sight of me or not."

Agreeing to this, the tiger accompanied him, and all other beasts who saw them coming dashed away. Not realizing that it was him they feared, the tiger thought they were afraid of the fox.

狐假虎威

虎求百兽而食之,得狐。

狐曰:"子无敢食我也!天帝使我长百兽①。今子食我,是逆天帝命也②!——子以我为不信?吾为子先行,子随我后,观百兽之见我而敢不走乎?"

虎以为然,故遂与之行。兽见之皆走。虎不知兽畏己而走也,以为畏狐也。

① 长百兽:做百兽之王。
② 逆:违背,违抗。

The Snipe and the Mussel

A mussel was opening its shell to bask in the sun when a snipe took a peck at it. The mussel clamped down on the bird's beak and held it fast.

"If it doesn't rain today or tomorrow," said the snipe, "there will be a dead mussel lying here."

"If I don't set you free today or tomorrow," retorted the mussel, "there will be a dead snipe here too."

As neither would give way, a fisherman came and caught them both.

鹬蚌相争①

……蚌方出曝②,而鹬啄其肉,蚌合而拑其喙③。

鹬曰:"今日不雨,明日不雨,即有死蚌!"

蚌亦谓鹬曰:"今日不出,明日不出,即有死鹬!"

两者不肯相舍④,渔者得而并禽之⑤。

① 鹬(yù 域):水鸟名,头圆大,嘴长二三寸,全体黄褐色,胸腹白色,趾长无蹼,常栖水田中,捕食小昆虫。
② 曝:晒太阳。
③ 喙(huì 会):鸟嘴。
④ 舍:舍弃。
⑤ 禽:同"擒",捉住。

英汉对照
English-Chinese
中国文学宝库
Gems of Chinese Literature
古代文学系列
Classical Literature

The Wolf of Zhongshan

   Zhao Jianzi made a great hunt in Zhongshan with huntsmen leading the way and an array of hawks and hounds in the rear. Countless sprightly birds and savage beasts had fallen to his bowstring, when a wolf reared up human-fashion in his path, howling. Jianzi spat on his hands and mounted his chariot with his bow, Crowcaller, in his grasp, drew back a Manchurian arrot to his armpit and loosed it so that its flight drank blood. With a weird cry the wolf made off, and Jianzi drove after in angry pursuit, the dust he stirred up so curtaining the sky and his hoofbeats ringing so thunderously that from ten paces none could tell man from horse.

   The Mohist philosopher Dongguo, on his way north to Zhongshan to seek employment, had set out early and lost his way, whipping the donkey that faltered under its load of books. His heart pounded when he saw the cloud of dust, and all at once the wolf was upon him.

   "Oh sir!" it cried, craning its neck towards him, "does none aspire to succour his fellow creature? The turtle that Mao Bao set free took him across the river, and the snake that the Marquis of Sui spared won him a pearl. Surely a wolf is more resourceful than these. Will you not in my present plight pop me into your bag to eke out for a space my dying

中山狼传

赵简子大猎于中山①。虞人②导前,鹰犬罗后,捷禽鸷兽③,应弦而倒者不可胜数。有狼当道,人立而啼。简子唾手登车④,援乌号之弓⑤,挟肃慎之矢,一发饮羽,狼失声而逋⑥。简子怒,驱车逐之。惊尘蔽天,足音鸣雷,十步之外,不辨人马。

时,墨者东郭先生⑦,将北适中山以干仕⑧。策蹇驴⑨,囊图书,夙行失道⑩,望尘惊悸。狼奄至⑪,引首顾曰:"先生岂有志于济物哉?昔毛宝放龟而得渡,隋侯救蛇而获珠,蛇龟固弗灵于狼也。今日之事,何不使我得早处囊中以苟延残喘乎?异时倘得脱颖而出,先生

---

① 中山:今河北省定县一带。
② 虞人:主管山林、狩猎的官。
③ 鸷兽:凶猛的野兽。
④ 唾手登车:从容上车。
⑤ 援:手拉。
⑥ 逋(bū):逃跑。
⑦ 墨者:信仰墨子学说的人。
⑧ 干仕:谋求官职。
⑨ 蹇:跛腿。
⑩ 夙(sù)行失道:早晨赶路迷失了道路。夙,早晨。
⑪ 奄至:突然到来。

英汉对照
English-Chinese
中国文学宝库
Gems of Chinese Literature
古代文学系列
Classical Literature

The Wolf of Zhongshan

gasps? At large again, I will be more indebted than any snake or turtle to your compassion, which will have lent new life to the flesh on my expiring bones!"

"Aha!" said Dongguo, "but what are rewards, may I ask, against the incalculable calamity of giving offence to a powerful noble of ministerial lineage, which I risk if I harbour you, wolf? And yet Mozi's doctrine of universal love is sovereign; I must, I find, save you after all. The calamity must be." And so he unloaded his books from the bag and with much hesitation and circumspection began to pack the wolf inside, taking great care not to tread on its dewlap or trap its tail. He still had not succeeded after several tries, and its pursuers were drawing ever nearer.

"I am hard pressed, sir," pleaded the wolf, "and here are you fending off fire and flood with courtesy, fleeing brigands with car bells clanging when quick thought is the thing!" So Dongguo tucked in the wolf's feet and bound them with a cord, drawing its head down to its tail until it was curled like a hedgehog, bent like an inchworm, coiled like a snake and was as still as a tortoise. To all of this the wolf submitted, while Dongguo did as the wolf had directed and put it into the bag, which he then fastened and lifted with his shoulder on to the donkey, which he led off the road to the left to await the arrival of Zhao's men.

Jianzi was not long in coming, fuming with anger at the loss of the wolf. Drawing his sword, he lopped off the end of his chariot pole and showed it to Dongguo.

之恩,生死而肉骨也。敢不努力以效龟蛇之诚!"

先生曰:"嘻!私汝狼以犯世卿,忤权贵,祸且不测,敢望报乎?然墨之道,'兼爱'为本,吾终当有以活汝。脱有祸①,固所不辞也。"乃出图书,空囊橐,徐徐焉实狼其中,前虞跋胡,后恐疐尾②,三纳之而未克。徘徊容与③,追者益近,狼请曰:"事急矣!先生果将揖逊救焚溺,而鸣銮避寇盗耶?惟先生速图!"乃跼蹐四足④,引绳而束缚之,下首至尾,曲脊掩胡,蝟缩蠖屈,蛇盘龟息,以听命先生。先生如其指⑤,内狼于囊,遂括囊口,肩举驴上,引避道左,以待赵人之过。

已而简子至,求狼弗得,盛怒,拔剑斩辕端示先生,骂曰:"敢讳狼方向者,有如此辕!"

---

① 脱:即使,倘使。
② 疐:压住。
③ 容与:缓慢的样子。
④ 跼蹐(jújí):缩作一团,卷曲。
⑤ 如其指:按照它的意思做。指,同"旨"。

英汉对照
English-Chinese
中国文学宝库
Gems of Chinese Literature
古代文学系列
Classical Literature

21

"Thus will deal," he raged, "with any that conceal the path of the wolf!"

"My lord," began Dongguo, sinking meekly to the ground and shuffling forward on his knees, "I am but a simple man come in such haste from afar to make my way in the world that I am myself lost and have no means of tracking wolves for your lordship's hawks and hounds. Sheep, we are told, may stray upon many a byway despite docility that a boy may rule. Sheep are no match for a wolf, and there is no end to the byways of Zhongshan where they may stray. Scour the roads as I might I would but watch tree trunks for dead rabbits and cast my line in the branches. Rather ask your fur-capped huntsmen, whose province the chase is, than berate a wayfarer who, though stupid, knows at least that your wolf is a savage, rapacious beast at one with the jackal in his cruelty. If your lordship has the power to rid us of such, I shall of course do what little I can to help. Would I conceal the wolf and not speak up?"

Without a word, Jianzi drove back on to the road, while Dongguo rode on at twice his previous speed.

It was long before the last of the plumes and pennants passed away and the sound of chariots and horses was still. When the wolf reckoned that Jianzi was far away, it spoke up inside the bag.

"Take care, sir, and let me out. Loose my bonds and pluck the arrow from my foreleg, for I must be gone." Dongguo set to and released the wolf. "I am glad you saved me just now,

先生伏质就地,匍匐以进,跽①而言曰:"鄙人不慧,将有志于世。奔走遐方,自迷正途,又安能发狼踪以指示夫子之鹰犬也?然尝闻之,'大道以多歧亡羊'。夫羊,一童子可制之,如是其驯也,尚以多歧而亡;狼非羊比,而中山之歧可以亡羊者何限?乃区区循大道以求之,不几于守株缘木乎?况田猎,虞人之所事也,请君问诸皮冠②。行道之人何罪哉?且鄙人虽愚,独不知夫狼乎?性贪而狠,党豺为虐,君能除之,固当窥左足以效微劳,又肯讳之而不言哉?"简子默然,回车就道,先生亦驱驴兼程前进。

良久,羽旄之影渐没,车马之音不闻。狼度简子之去远,而作声囊中曰:"先生可留意矣,出我囊,解我缚,拔矢我臂,我将逝矣。"先

---

① 跽:挺直腰跪着。
② 皮冠:指管山泽、狩猎的官吏。

sir," it growled, "when the huntsmen pursued me and were likely soon to be upon me. But I must die now for all that, so famished I am, famished and foodless. Better to fall at the huntsmen's hands, a dainty for nobles, than to starve on the road and feed the beasts. A Mohist such as yourself, sir, who would be mauled form head to heel for the good of the world, surely would not begrudge his body, if his extinction afforded me a meal?" And it advanced on Dongguo, snarling and waggling its claws. Hurriedly Dongguo fended it off and retreated to shelter behind the donkey. Round and round they ran, the wolf never gaining on Dongguo, who defended himself with all his might, till both were panting with exhaustion on either side of the donkey.

"You deceived me! You deceived me!" said Dongguo.

"There was no deception intended on my part," said the wolf. "The fact is that Heaven created your kind to be eaten by mine." They both held out while the shadows inexorably shifted.

"The day draws to evening," thought Dongguo, "and when the wolf pack arrives I shall be a dead man indeed!" He decided to trick the wolf. "It is a popular custom," he said, "that moot questions be referred to three elders. Let us go now and seek out three to ask. If they say I am to be eaten, I will be eaten; if not, let that be an end of it."

This pleased the wolf greatly, and they set off together at once.

They had walked for some time along empty roads when

生举手出狼。狼咆哮谓先生曰:"适为虞人逐,其来甚速,幸先生生我。我馁甚,馁不得食,亦终必亡而已。与其饥死道路,为群兽食,毋宁毙于虞人,以俎豆于贵家①。先生既墨者,摩顶放踵,思一利天下,又何吝一躯啖我,而全微命乎?"遂鼓吻奋爪,以向先生。

先生仓卒以手搏之,且搏且却,引蔽驴后,便旋而走。狼终不得有加于先生,先生亦竭力拒,彼此俱倦,隔驴喘息。先生曰:"狼负我!狼负我!"狼曰:"吾非固欲负汝,天生汝辈,固需吾辈食也。"相持既久,日暮游移②,先生窃念,天色向晚,狼复群至,吾死矣夫!因绐③狼曰:"民俗,事疑必询三老④,第行矣⑤,求三老而问之,苟谓我可食即食,不可即已。"狼大喜,即与偕行。

---

① 俎豆:俎(zǔ)和豆都是古时祭祀时盛祭品的器具。
② 日暮(guǐ):日影。
③ 绐(dài):哄骗。
④ 三老:古代掌教化的乡官,这里指有德行的老年人。
⑤ 第:但,只管。

英汉对照
English-Chinese
中国文学宝库
Gems of Chinese Literature
古代文学系列
Classical Literature

the wolf, which was becoming ravenous, spied an old tree standing stiffly by the wayside.

"There is an elder to ask," it said to Dongguo.

"What is the point of putting it to a plant?" asked Dongguo. "They have no senses."

"Go ahead and ask," said the wolf. "It will speak, I think." There was nothing for it but for Dongguo to bow politely to the old tree and lay the entire matter before it.

"Should I," he concluded, "under the circumstances, be eaten?"

A rumbling came from within the tree.

"I," it began, "am an apricot tree. Years ago, when the gardener planted me, the only expense involved was one stone. A year later I flowered, and the next year I bore fruit. After three years I was two hand spans in girth, after ten two arm spans. Now, twenty years later, I have fed the gardener and his wife and their guests and servants too. He has even sold my fruit on the market to make money. I must have been of enormous use to him, but now that I am old I can no longer make my flowers wither into fruit, and this makes him angry, so that he breaks off my twigs, lops my leafy branches and is going to sell me to a carpenter to turn a profit. Life's shadows are lengthening, and I am so much coarse timber, with no prospect of escaping the sentence of the axe, so why should you expect to escape now that you are of no use to the wolf? Yes, you should be eaten."

At these words the wolf again advanced on Dongguo,

逾时，道无行人。狼馋甚，望老木僵立路侧，谓先生曰："可问是老。"先生曰："草木无知，叩焉何益？"狼曰："第问之，彼当有言矣！"先生不得已，揖老木具述始末；问曰："若然，狼当食我耶？"木中轰轰有声，谓先生曰："我，杏也。往年老圃种我时，费一核耳，逾年华①，再逾年实②，三年拱把③，十年合抱，至于今二十年矣，老圃食我，老圃之妻子食我。外至宾客，下至于仆，皆食我。又复鬻实于市以规利。我其有功于老圃甚巨。今老矣，不得敛华就实④，贾老圃怒，伐我条枚，芟我枝叶，且将售我工师之肆取直焉⑤。噫！樗朽之材⑥，桑榆之景⑦，求免于斧钺之诛而不可得。汝何德于狼，乃觊免乎？是固当食汝。"言下，狼复鼓吻奋爪，以向先生。先生曰："狼爽盟矣；矢⑧

① 华：开花。
② 实：结果。
③ 拱把：两手相合那么粗。
④ 敛华就实：落花结果。
⑤ 取直：换钱。
⑥ 樗朽：樗(shù)，一种叫臭椿的树，木质粗松。
⑦ 桑榆：指日落的地方，用来比喻晚年。
⑧ 矢：发誓，保证。

英汉对照
English-Chinese
中国文学宝库
Gems of Chinese Literature
古代文学系列
Classical Literature

snarling and waggling its claws.

"You are breaking our pact," said Dongguo, "which was to consult three elders. I will not succumb on the strength of one apricot tree."

They set off again together.

The wolf, ever more eager, spied an old cow sunning itself behind a ruined wall.

"There is an elder to ask," it said to Dongguo.

"What point is there," said Dongguo, "in asking a cow, a mere animal, any more than the senseless plant we asked just now that told such malicious falsehoods?"

"Go ahead and ask," said the wolf, "unless you want to feel my teeth." There was nothing for it but for Dongguo to bow politely to the cow and lay the entire matter before her. She frowned and stared, then opened her mouth and licked her nose.

"The things the old apricot tree told you," she said, "were no malicious falsehoods. I am an old cow, but in my youth my sinews were so strong that the farmer bartered a sword for me and put me to work in the south field with the oxen. I was sturdy and they were failing, so that the work eventually all fell on me. When he wanted to drive, I would bend to the bunting carriage, and how we would bowl along on the good roads! And when he wanted to do the ploughing, off would come my yoke and away we would go to the fields to root out the hazel trees and the thorn bushes. He cared for me as he cared for his own two hands. It was I who fed and clothed

询三老,今值一杏,何遽见迫耶?"复与偕行。

狼愈急,望见老牸①,曝日败垣中,谓先生曰:"可问是老。"先生曰:"向者草木无知,谬言害事,今牛,禽兽耳,更何问为?"狼曰:"第问之,不问将咥汝②。"先生不得已,揖老牸,再述始末以问,牛皱眉瞪目,舐鼻张口,向先生曰:"老杏之言不谬矣。老牸茧栗少年时,筋力颇健,老农卖一刀以易我,使我贰群牛,事南亩。既壮,群牛日以老惫,凡事我都任之。

① 老牸(zì):老母牛。
② 咥(dié):咬。

him, I who got him married, I who paid his taxes and I who filled his granaries. I expected nothing but the shelter as his horses and dogs did. He used not to keep a hundredweight of wheat, and now he harvests ten tons extra; he used to live too miserably to look for a loan, and now he idles in the marketplace; for half his life his cups and bottles gathered dust and he never wiped his parched lips from a full wine jar, and now he brews sorghum and millet and raises flagons to the honour of his womenfolk; his clothes were skimpy homespun, his cronies were trees and rocks, and he never had the courtesy for a bow or the mind to study — whereas now he carries books, wears a bamboo hat and girds his flowing robes with a leather belt. Every thread and every grain of that is my labour, but now that I am old and weak he has cheated me and driven me out into the field, where the aching wind lashes my eyes as I complain to my shadow on cold days, a thin mountain of bone raining old tears, with a drooling mouth I cannot stop, cramped limbs I cannot lift, a hide devoid of hair and running sores that will not heal. The farmer's wife is brazenly jealous too, urging him on night and day, 'There's no waste on a cow,' she says. 'The meat can be dried; the hide can be tanned; even the bones and horns can be cut up and polished to make things.' 'You,' she says to her eldest boy, 'you have worked for the butcher for years. Why don't you sharpen your knives and slaughter her? I see no good coming of this for me. I could be dead at any moment. Well, that is the way of it. They have no gratitude,

彼将驰驱,我伏田车,择便途以急奔趋;彼将躬耕,我脱辐衡,走郊坰以辟榛荆① 老农亲我②,犹左右手。衣食仰我而给,婚姻仰我而毕,赋税仰我而输,仓庾仰我而实。我亦自谅,可得帷席之蔽如马狗也。往年家储无儋石③,今麦收多十斛矣;往年穷居无顾借,今掉臂行村社矣;往年尘卮罂,涸唇吻,盛酒瓦盆,半生未接,今酝黍稷,据尊罍,骄妻妾矣;往年衣短褐,侣木石,手不知揖,心不知学,今持兔园册④,戴笠子,腰韦带,衣宽博矣。一丝一粟,皆我力也。顾欺我老弱,逐我郊野,酸风射眸⑤,寒日吊影,瘦骨如山,老泪如雨,涎垂而不可收,足挛而不可举;皮毛俱亡,疮痍未瘥⑥。老农之妻妒且悍,朝夕进说曰:'牛之一身无废物也:肉可脯,皮可鞟,骨、角且切磋为器。'指大儿曰:'汝受业庖丁之门有年矣,胡不砺刃于硎以待⑦?'迹是观之,是将不利于我,我不知死所矣。夫我有功,彼无情,乃若

---

① 坰(jiǒng):郊野。榛荆:野草杂树。
② 亲我:依靠我。
③ 儋(dàn)石:一石为石,两石为儋。
④ 兔园册:即《兔园策》,一种启蒙读物。《五代史·刘岳传》:"兔园策者乡校里儒教田夫牧子之所诵也。"
⑤ 酸风射眸:冷风刺眼。眸,眼珠。
⑥ 瘥:瘥(chāi),痊愈。
⑦ 硎:硎(xíng),磨刀石。

英汉对照
English-Chinese
中国文学宝库
Gems of Chinese Literature
古代文学系列
Classical Literature

so I must suffer. Why should you have the luck to escape now that you are of no use to the wolf?" At this the wolf once more advanced on Dongguo, snarling and waggling its claws.

"Not so fast!" said Dongguo.

From the distance an old man could be seen approaching, leaning on a staff of black hellebore. His beard and eyebrows were snowy white, and this, together with the casual refinement of his dress, gave him an air of respectability. With a mixture of delight and amazement, Dongguo went ahead of the wolf and threw himself on his knees, sobbing.

"Oh, sir," he began ruefully, "one word from you can save my life!"

"In what way?" asked the old man.

"When this wolf was at the mercy of huntsmen it begged me to save it, and I did. Now it wants to eat me and will not be swayed by my pleas. Thinking to delay my doom, I had it swear to let three elders decide. First we came upon an old apricot tree, which the wolf forced me to ask, and the senseless plant was almost the death of me. Next we came upon an old cow, and the wolf forced me to ask her. She was nearly the death of me too. Now, sir, there is you. In Heaven's name, sir, preserve me! Pronounce, I implore you, the words that will save my life!" He struck his head on the ground at the base of the staff and awaited his judgment, prone.

The old man heard him out, sucked his teeth for some time, then rapped the wolf with his staff.

是行将蒙祸;汝何德于狼,觊幸免乎?"言下,狼又鼓吻奋爪以向先生。先生曰:"毋欲速!"

遥望老子杖藜而来,须眉皓然,衣冠闲雅,盖有道者也。先生且喜且愕,舍狼而前,拜跪啼泣,致辞曰:"乞丈人一言而生。"丈人问故,先生曰:"是狼为虞人所窘,求救于我,我实生之。今反欲咥我,力求不免,我又当死之。欲少延于片时,誓定是于三老。初逢老杏,强我问之,草木无知几杀我。次逢老牸,强我问之,禽兽无知,又将杀我。今逢丈人,岂天之未丧斯文也?敢乞一言而生!"而顿首杖下,俯伏听命。丈人闻之,唏嘘再三,以杖叩狼曰:"汝

"You are wrong!" he said. " There is no worse sign than ingratitude. Wise men tell us that the impulse to gratitude is what makes dutiful child, and we are also told that tigers and wolves have family feelings. You, though, seem to have none, such is your ingratitude. Begone," he bellowed. "before I slay you with this staff!"

"You know only the one side of it, sir," replied the wolf. "If you care to listen, I will explain. In order to save me, he bound my legs and shut me in his bag with so many books of poetry on top of me that I could scarcely breathe. And then he prattles and prates away to Jianzi as if he wants me to die in his bag and take all the credit himself. Why should I not eat him after that?"

"Even Yi the Great Archer was wrong to do such a thing," said the old man, turning to Dongguo, who indignantly explained that he had put the wolf in the bag out of compassion, while the wolf replied with subtle arguments to win its point.

"None of this is at all convincing, " said the old man. "The only way that I can see whether any suffering was caused is to put the wolf back into the bag." The wolf agreed readily and held out its feet to Dongguo, who bound it again, put it in the bag and shouldered it up on to the donkey before the wolf realized what was happening.

"Have you a dagger?" the old man whispered in Dongguo's ear.

误矣!夫人有恩而背之,不祥莫大焉。儒谓受人恩而不忍背者,其为子必孝,又谓虎狼之父子。今汝背恩如是,则并父子亦无矣。"乃厉声曰:"狼速去,不然,将杖杀汝。"

狼曰:"丈人知其一,未知其二,请愬之,愿丈人垂听。初,先生救我时,束缚我足,闭我囊中,压以诗书,我鞠躬不敢息,又蔓词以说简子,其意盖将死我于囊而独窃其利也,是安可不咥?"丈人顾先生曰:"果如是,是羿亦有罪焉。"先生不平,具状其囊狼怜惜之意。狼亦巧辩不已以求胜。丈人曰:"是皆不足以执信也。试再囊之,吾观其状果困苦否。"狼欣然从之,信足先生① 先生复缚置囊中,肩举驴上,而狼未之知也。丈人附耳谓先生曰:"有匕首

---

① 信:信(shēn),同"伸"。

"Yes," said Dongguo, taking it out. The old man indicated with a glance that Dongguo should draw the dagger and stab the wolf.

"Harm it?" said Dongguo. "Surely not!"

"If you cannot bring yourself to kill a brute that has repaid your kindness in this fashion, you are indeed a man of compassion," laughed the old man, "and also an utter fool! Surely you are not one of those who risk all by thinking only of others, leaping into wells to save them and going naked to preserve your neighbours? Foolishness is the vice of kindness, and a true man has no part of it." And he laughed so loudly that Dongguo began to laugh too. Then the old man raised his hand and helped him wield the blade, and together they slew the wolf, cast it by the roadside and went their way.

否?"先生曰:"有。"于是出匕,丈人目先生使引匕刺狼。先生曰:"不害狼夫?"丈人笑曰:"禽兽负恩如是,而犹不忍杀,子固仁者,然愚亦甚矣!从井以救人,解衣以活友,于彼计则得,其如就死地何?先生其此类乎?仁陷于愚,固君子之所不与也。"言已大笑,先生亦笑,遂举手助先生操刃共殪狼,弃道上而去。

英汉对照
English-Chinese
中国文学宝库
Gems of Chinese Literature
古代文学系列
Classical Literature

Entering the City Gate with a Long Pole

In the land of Lu a man with a long pole wanted to pass through the city gate. First he held the pole vertically but could not pass; then he held it horizontally but could not get through either. He was at a loss.

Then an old man truned up and said, "I am not a sage, but I've had plenty of experience. Why not cut your pole into two to enter the city?"

So the fellow cut the pole as he was told.

截竿入城①

鲁有执长竿入城门者,初竖执之,不可入;横执之,亦不可入,计无所出。

俄有老父至曰:"吾非圣人,但见事多矣。何不以锯中截而入②?"

遂依而截之。

---

① 截竿入城:截断竹竿进城。
② 中截:从中间截断。

Punishing the Horse

Because his horse refused to advance, a traveller in the state of Song drove it into a stream, then mounted to set off again. Still the horse refused to go, and he punished it once more in the same way. This happened three times in all. Even the most skilful rider could devise no better means of frightening a horse; but if you are not a rider, simply a bully, your horse will refuse to carry you.

取道杀马

宋人有取①道者,其马不进,倒而投②之瀫水③。又复取道,其马不进,又倒而投之瀫水。如此三者。虽造父④之所以威马不过此矣。不得造父之道,而徒得其威,无益于御。

---

① 取:即"趋",赶路。
② 投:投入,这里可当"赶进"讲。
③ 瀫(xī)水:溪名。
④ 造父(fǔ):古代传说中最好的御手。

英汉对照
English-Chinese
中国文学宝库
Gems of Chinese Literature
古代文学系列
Classical Literature

Why Zeng Shen Killed the Pig

One day, when Zeng Shen's wife was going to the market, their son cried and clamoured to go with her.

"Go back now!" she wheedled him. "When I get home we'll kill the pig for you."

Upon her return, she found Zeng Shen about to kill the pig. She hastily stopped him.

"I didn't really mean it," she protested. "I just said that to keep the boy quiet."

"How can you deceive a child like that?" asked Zeng Shen. "Children know nothing to begin with, but they copy their parents and learn from them. When you cheat the boy, you are teaching him to lie. If a mother deceives her child, he will not trust her, and that is no way to bring him up."

So he killed the pig after all.

曾子杀猪

曾子①之妻之市,其子随之而泣。其母曰:"女还,顾反为女杀彘②。"

妻适③市来,曾子欲捕彘杀之,妻止之曰:"特④与婴儿戏耳。"曾子曰:"婴儿非与戏也。婴儿非有知也,待父母而学者也,听父母之教,今子欺之,是教子欺也。母欺子,子而不信其母,非所以成教也。"遂烹⑤彘也。

① 曾子:名参,字子舆,孔子的学生。
② 顾:只。彘(zhì):猪。
③ 适:往。
④ 特:只是。
⑤ 烹(pēng):烧煮食物。

英汉对照
English-Chinese
中国文学宝库
Gems of Chinese Literature
古代文学系列
Classical Literature

The Dog Who Soured Wine

There was a brewer in the state of Song whose wine was excellent. He gave fair measure, was civil to his customers, and had his sign up in a most conspicuous place. Yet he could not sell his wine, which was said to be sour. He asked an elder whom he knew well, what the reason for this was.

"Is your dog fierce?" asked the elderly man.

"As a matter of fact, it is," replied the brewer. "But what has that to do with my wine not selling?"

"People are afraid of your dog. When a boy is sent with money and a pot to buy your wine, the dog rushes out to bite him. That is why your wine turns sour and will not sell."

狗猛酒酸

宋人有酤酒者①,升概②甚平,遇客③甚谨,为酒甚美,悬帜甚高,著④然不售,酒酸。怪其故⑤,问其所知闾长者杨倩⑥。倩曰:"汝狗猛邪?"曰:"狗猛,则酒何故而不售?"曰:"人畏焉⑦。或令孺子怀钱挈壶瓮⑧而往酤,而狗迓而龁之⑨,此酒所以酸而不售也。"

夫国亦有狗。有道之士怀其术而欲以明万乘之主⑩,大臣为猛狗迎而龁之。此人主之所以蔽胁⑪,而有道之士所以不用也。

---

① 酤:同"沽",这里指卖酒;下文"往酤"的"酤",指买酒。
② 升:量器,古代用升斗作量酒的器具。概:平斗斛(hú,容器)的木棍。"升概"在这里指量酒。
③ 遇客:招待顾客。
④ 著(zhù):同"贮",积贮起来。
⑤ 怪其故:对于酒酸的缘故感到奇怪。
⑥ 闾(lǘ):里巷。长者:老年人。
⑦ 焉:代词,它,指狗。
⑧ 孺子:小孩。挈(qiè):携带。瓮(wèng):瓦壶。
⑨ 迓(yà):迎着。龁(hé):咬。
⑩ 有道之士:有才干的人。万乘之主:君王。
⑪ 蔽胁:蒙蔽,胁迫。

英汉对照
English-Chinese
中国文学宝库
Gems of Chinese Literature
古代文学系列
Classical Literature

Tht Use of Parables

"Hui Zi is forever using parables," complained someone to the Prince of Liang. "If you, sir, forbid him to speak in parables, he won't be able to make his meaning clear."

The prince agreed with this man.

The next day the prince saw Hui Zi.

"From now on," he said, "kindly talk in a straightforward manner, and not in parables."

"Suppose there were a man who did not know what a catapult is," replied Hui Zi. "If he asked you what it looked like, and you told him it looked just like a catapult, would he understand what you meant?"

"Of couse not," answered the prince.

"But suppose you told him that a catapult looks something like a bow and that it is made of bamboo — wouldn't he understand you better?"

"Yes, that would be clearer," admitted the prince.

"We compare something a man does not know with something he does know in order to help him to understand it," said Hui Zi. "If you won't let me use parables, how can I make things clear to you?"

The prince agreed that he was right.

惠子善譬

客谓梁王曰:"惠子之言事也善譬①。王使无譬②,则不能言矣。"王曰:"诺。"明日见,谓惠子曰:"愿先生言事则直言耳,无譬也。"惠子曰:"今有人于此而不知'弹'者,曰:'弹之状何若?'应曰:'弹之状如弹',则谕③乎?"王曰:"未谕也。""于是更应曰:'弹之状如弓,而以竹为弦,'则知乎?"王曰:"可知矣。"惠子曰:"夫说者固以其所知谕其所不知,而使人知之。今王曰无譬,则不可矣。"王曰:"善。"

① 善譬:会打比方。譬,比喻,比方。
② 无譬:不要打比方。
③ 谕:理解,明白。

英汉对照
English-Chinese
中国文学宝库
Gems of Chinese Literature
古代文学系列
Classical Literature

The Cicada, the Praying Mantis and the Sparrow

The Prince of Wu decided to attack the state of Chu. He gave a stern warning to his subjects that anyone who raised objections would be put to death.

One of his stewards wanted to protest, but dared not. Instead, he took a catapult and pellets and wandered in the back courtyard until his clothes were wet with dew. He did this for three mornings.

"Come here," ordered the prince. "What are you doing to make your clothes wet with dew?"

"There is a tree in the garden," replied the steward, and on it there is a cicada. This cicada perches up there, chirping away and drinking the dew, not knowing that there is a praying mantis behind it. And the praying mantis leans forward, raising its forelegs to catch the cicada, not knowing that there is a sparrow beside it. The sparrow, again, cranes its neck to peck at the praying mantis, not knowing that there is someone with a catapult waiting below. These three small creatures are so eager to profit by something directly in front of them that they fail to realize the danger behind."

"Well said," replied the prince, and he gave up his plan of invasion.

螳螂捕蝉

吴王欲伐荆①,告其左右曰:"敢有谏者死"。舍人有少孺子②者,欲谏不敢,则怀操弹于后园,露沾其衣,如是者三旦。吴王曰:"子来,何苦沾衣如此?"对曰:"园中有树,其上有蝉。蝉高居悲鸣饮露,不知螳螂在其后也;螳螂委身曲附③欲取蝉,而不知黄雀在其傍也;黄雀延颈欲啄螳螂,而不知弹丸在其下也。此三者皆务欲④得其前利,而不顾其后之有患也"。吴王曰:"善哉"。乃罢其兵。

---

① 荆:古荆州之地,指楚国。
② 少孺子:少年。
③ 委身曲附:把身子贴在隐秘的地方。
④ 务欲:力求想要。

英汉对照
English-Chinese
中国文学宝库
Gems of Chinese Literature
古代文学系列
Classical Literature

The Fur and the Hide

While on a tour of the country, Marquis Wen of the State of Wei saw a man wearing a fur with the hide outside, carrying a bundle of straw.

"Why wear your fur inside out to carry straw?" asked the marquis.

"To protect the fur," was the answer.

"Don't you realize, man," said the marquis, "that when the hide wears out, the fur will go too?"

反裘负刍

魏文侯出游,见路人反裘而负刍①,文侯曰:"胡为反裘而负刍?"对曰:"臣爱其毛。"文侯曰:"若不知其里尽而毛无所恃②邪?"

---

① 反裘而负刍:裘,皮衣;刍(chú),喂牲口的草。当时百姓穿羊皮的习惯是把羊毛露在外面,而这个人却把皮板露在外面,肩上拥着柴草。
② 恃:依靠,依附。

英汉对照
English-Chinese
中国文学宝库
Gems of Chinese Literature
古代文学系列
Classical Literature

The Man Who Lost His Jacket

There was a man called Cheng Zi in the land of Song. Having lost his black jacket, he went out to search the road for it. When he saw a woman wearing a black jacket, he seized her and would not let go, wanting her garment.

"I lost my black jacket today," he said.

"What if you did?" she retorted. "This black jacket is one I made with my own hands."

But Cheng Zi said, "You had better give it to me quickly. What I lost was a lined jacket, while this of yours is unlined. Isn't it to your advantage to exchange an unlined jacket for a lined one?"

澄子亡缁衣①

宋有澄子者,亡缁衣,求之涂②。见妇人衣缁衣,援而弗舍③,欲取其衣,曰:"今者我亡缁衣!"

妇人曰:"公虽亡缁衣,此实吾所自为也。"

澄子曰:"子不如速与我衣!昔吾所亡者纺缁也④,今子之衣禅缁也⑤。以禅缁当纺缁,子岂不得哉⑥!"

---

① 澄子:人名。亡:丢失。缁(zī资)衣:黑色的衣服。
② 涂:同"途"。
③ 援:牵,扯。
④ 纺缁:指夹的黑衣。纺,复。
⑤ 禅(dān单)缁:单的黑衣。禅,单衣。
⑥ 得:便宜。

英汉对照
English-Chinese
中国文学宝库
Gems of Chinese Literature
古代文学系列
Classical Literature

The Owl Moves House

The owl met the turtle-dove. "Where are you going?" inquired the dove.

"I am moving east," said the owl.

"Why is that?" asked the dove.

"All the people here dislike my hoot," replied the owl. "That is why I want to move east."

"If you can change your voice, well and good," said the dove. "But if you can't, even if you move east the people there will dislike you just the same."

枭将东徙①

枭逢鸠②。
鸠曰:"子将安之③?"
枭曰:"我将东徙。"
鸠曰:"何故?"
枭曰:"乡人皆恶我鸣④,以故东徙。"
鸠曰:"子能更鸣⑤,可矣。不能更鸣,东徙犹恶子之声。"

---

① 枭(xiāo 消)将东徙:猫头鹰要搬到东方去住。枭,猫头鹰。
② 鸠:斑鸠。
③ 安之:到何处去。
④ 恶(wù 物):厌恶、讨厌。
⑤ 更(gēng 庚):改变。

Buying a Pair of Shoes

A man in the State of Zheng decided to buy himself a pair of shoes. He measured his feet but left the measure on his seat, and went to the market without it. When he found the shoes he wanted, he gave an exclamation of dismay:

"Why, I forgot to bring the measurement!"

He hurried home to fetch it.

By the time he got back to the market, the fair was over; so he failed to buy his shoes.

"Why didn't you try the shoes on?" someone asked him.

"I trust the ruler more than my feet," was his reply.

郑人买履

郑人有欲买履者①,先自度其足②,而置之其坐③。

至之市④,而忘操之。已得履,乃曰:"吾忘持度。"

反归取之。

及反,市罢,遂不得履。

人曰:"何不试之以足?"

曰:"宁信度,无自信也。"

---

① 履(lǚ 吕):鞋。
② 度其足:指记下脚的尺码。度,量。
③ 坐:同"座"。
④ 至之市:去到集市。

英汉对照
English-Chinese
中国文学宝库
Gems of Chinese Literature
古代文学系列
Classical Literature

Marking the Boat to Locate the Sword

A man was ferrying across a river when his sword fell into the water. He lost no time in marking the side of the boat.

"What use is it making a mark there?" someone asked.

"This is where my sword dropped," he said. When the boat moored, he got into the water to look for his sword by the place he had marked.

But since the boat had moved while the sword had not, this method of locating his sword proved unsuccessful.

刻舟求剑

楚人有涉江者,其剑自舟中坠于水,遽契其舟①,曰:"是吾剑之所从坠。"

舟止,从其所契者入水求之。

舟已行矣,而剑不行,求剑若此,不亦惑乎②?

---

① 遽契:急忙刻下记号。契,刻。
② 惑:迷惑。

Too Many Paths

One of Yang Zi's neighbours, who lost a sheep, sent all his men out to find it, and asked Yang Zi's servant to join in the search.

"What!" exclaimed Yang Zi. "Do you need all those men to find one sheep?"

"There are so many paths it may have taken," the neighbour explained.

When his servant returned, Yang Zi asked him: "Well, did you find the sheep?"

He answered that they had not. Then Yang Zi asked how they had failed to find it.

"There are too many paths," replied the servant. "One path leads to another, and we didn't know which to take, so we had to come back."

At that Yang Zi looked very thoughtful. He was silent for a long time, and did not smile all day.

His pupils were surprised.

"A sheep is a trifle," they said, "and this wasn't even yours. Why should you stop talking and smiling?"

Yang Zi did not answer, and his pupils were puzzled.

多歧亡羊

杨子之邻人亡羊①。既率其党,又请杨子之竖追之②。

杨子曰:"嘻!亡一羊,何追者之众?"邻人曰:"多歧路③。"

既反,问:"获羊乎?"曰:"亡之矣"。曰:"奚④亡之?"曰:"歧路之中又有歧焉,吾不知所之⑤,所以反也。"

杨子戚然变容,不言者移时,不笑者竟日⑥。门人怪之⑦,请曰:"羊贱畜,又非夫子之有,而损⑧言笑者,何哉?"杨子不答。门人不获所命⑨。

---

① 杨子:即杨朱,战国时哲学家,宣扬拔一毛而利天下都不为的利己主义哲学。亡:走失。
② 既:已经。党:家属亲族。竖(shù):家僮。
③ 歧(qí):岔路。
④ 奚(xī):怎么。
⑤ 所之:去的地方。
⑥ 戚:忧伤。移时:历时,经时,这里指半晌。竟日:终日。
⑦ 门人怪之:即门人以之为怪。门人,学生。
⑧ 损:减少。
⑨ 所命:答案,含意。

英汉对照
English-Chinese
中国文学宝库
Gems of Chinese Literature
古代文学系列
Classical Literature

Presenting Doves

It was the custom in Handan to catch doves to present to the prince on New Year's Day, for this pleased him so much that he gave rich rewards. Somenone asked the prince the reason for this custom.

"I free the doves at New Year to show my kindness," he said.

"Since your subjects know you want doves to set free, they all set about catching them," objected the other. "And the result is that many doves are killed. If you really want to save the doves, you had better forbid people to catch them. As things are, you catch them to free them, and your kindness cannot make up for the damage you do."

The prince agreed with him.

献 鸠

邯郸之民①,以正月之旦②,献鸠于简子③,简子大悦,厚赏之。

客问其故。

简子曰:"正旦放生,示有恩也。"

客曰:"民知君之欲放之,竞而捕之,死者众矣。君如欲生之,不若禁民勿捕;捕而放之,恩过不相补矣④。"

简子曰:"然。"

---

① 邯郸:战国时赵国国都。即今河北省邯郸市。
② 正月之旦:正月初一那一天。
③ 简子:即赵简子。
④ 补:补偿。

Felling the Plane Tree

A man had a withered plane tree.

"It's unlucky to keep a withered tree," said his neighbour.

But when the first man had felled the tree, his neighbour asked him for some of the wood as fuel.

"The old man simply wanted some fuel," thought the owner of the tree indignantly. "That's why he told me to fell my tree. We are neighbours, and yet he tricks me in this way — this is really going too far!"

枯梧不祥[①]

人有枯梧树者,其邻父言枯梧之树不祥,其邻人遽而伐之[②]。

邻人父固请以为薪[③]。

其人乃不悦曰:"邻人之父徒欲为薪,而教吾伐之也。与我邻若此,其险岂可哉!"

[①] 枯梧不祥:枯干了的梧桐树不吉利。
[②] 其邻人:疑"邻"字衍,当为"其人"。《吕氏春秋·去宥》亦载此事云:"邻人遽伐之,邻父因请而以为薪。"其文意不同,是说邻人砍伐的,邻父因此要求当柴烧。
[③] 邻人父:疑"人"字衍,当为"邻父"。

英汉对照
English-Chinese
中国文学宝库
Gems of Chinese Literature
古代文学系列
Classical Literature

The Man Who Saw Nobody

There was a man in the State of Qi who wanted some gold. One morning he dressed himself smartly and went to the market. Arriving at the gold-dealer's stall, he seized a piece of gold and made off.

The officer who caught him asked him: " Why did you steal gold in front of so many people?"

"When I took the gold," he answered, "I saw nobody. All I saw was the gold."

攫 金①

昔齐人有欲金者②,清旦衣冠而之市③,适鬻金者之所④,因攫其金而去。

吏捕得之。问曰:"人皆在焉,子攫人之金何?"

对曰:"取金之时,不见人,徒见金⑤!"

---

① 攫(jué 决)金:抢夺人家的金子。
② 欲:欲望、企望、想要。
③ 清旦:早晨。
④ 鬻(yù 欲):卖。
⑤ 徒:只、但。

英汉对照
English-Chinese
中国文学宝库
Gems of Chinese Literature
古代文学系列
Classical Literature

The Ointment for Chapped Hands

A family in the State of Song made an excellent ointment for chapped hands; so for generations they engaged in laundering. A man who heard of this offered a hundred pieces of gold for their recipe.

"We have been in the laundry trade for generations," said this family as they discussed the matter. "But we never made more than a few pieces of gold. Today we can sell our recipe for a hundred pieces. By all means let us sell it."

Now the State of Yue was invading the State of Wu, and having bought the recipe this man presented it to the Prince of Wu, who thereupon made him a general. His troops fought a naval action with those of Yue that winter, and completely routed the enemy. Then the prince made him a noble, rewarding him with a fief.

Thus the same ointment for chaps could win a fief or simply aid laundrymen. All depends upon the use to which things are put.

不龟手之药①

宋人有善为不龟手之药者,世世以洴澼絖为事②。客闻之,请买其方百金③。聚族而谋曰:"我世世为洴澼絖,不过数金,今一朝而鬻技百金④,请与之。"

客得之,以说吴王。越有难,吴王使之将⑤。冬,与越人水战,大败越人,裂地而封之⑥。

能不龟手一也,或以封,或不免于洴澼絖,则所用之异也。

---

① 不龟手之药:擦在手上可以防冻的药。不龟手,即不皲(jūn 军)手。皲,手足皮肤受冻而坼裂。
② 洴澼絖(píng pì kuàng 平僻矿):在水上漂洗绵絮。洴澼,漂洗击絮的声音。絖,是絮,丝绵。
③ 百金:金方寸重一斤为一金;百金,百斤黄金。
④ 鬻技:用不龟手之药的秘方卖钱。鬻,卖。
⑤ 将(jiàng 酱):将领、统帅军队。
⑥ 裂地而封:割地封侯。

英汉对照
English-Chinese
中国文学宝库
Gems of Chinese Literature
古代文学系列
Classical Literature

The Bird Killed by Kindness

A seagull alighted in a suburb of the capital of Lu. The Marquis of Lu welcomed it and feasted it in the temple hall, ordering the best music and grandest sacrifices for it. But the bird remained in a daze, looking quite wretched, not daring to swallow a morsel of meat or a single cup of wine. And after three days it died.

This was entertaining the seagull as the Marquis of Lu liked to be entertained, not as a seagull likes to be entertained.

鲁侯养鸟

昔者海鸟止于鲁郊,鲁侯御而觞之于庙①,奏《九韶》以为乐②,具太牢以为膳③。

鸟乃眩视忧悲④,不敢食一脔⑤,不敢饮一杯,三日而死。

此以己养养鸟也,非以鸟养养鸟也。

---

① 御:迎。觞(shāng 伤):献酒。
② 《九韶》:古代乐曲名。
③ 太牢:古代帝王、诸侯祭祀社稷时,牛、羊、猪三牲全备为"太牢"。亦作"大牢"。
④ 眩(xuàn 炫)视:目光昏花。
⑤ 脔(luán 峦):切成块的肉。

英汉对照
English-Chinese
中国文学宝库
Gems of Chinese Literature
古代文学系列
Classical Literature

Learning the Wrong Thing

Because Xi Shi, the famous beauty, suffered from heartburn, she would often frown in front of all the neighbours.

An ugly girl in the same village, who noticed this and thought it very charming, also put her hands to her breast and frowned in front of everyone. When the rich saw her, they barred their doors and would not come out. As for the poor, they ran away, taking their wives and children.

Poor thing! She could admire Xi Shi's frown, but did not know why it was beautiful.

丑女效颦①

西施病心而矉②。

其里之丑人,见而美之,归亦捧心而矉。

其里之富人见之,坚闭门而不出;贫人见之,挈妻子而去之走③。

彼知矉美,而不知矉之所以美。

---

① 颦(pín 贫):皱眉头。
② 病心:害心痛病。实是胃痛。矉(pín 贫):同"颦",蹙着眉毛。
③ 挈(qiè 窃):携带。

英汉对照
English-Chinese
中国文学宝库
Gems of Chinese Literature
古代文学系列
Classical Literature

The Frog in the Well

A frog lived in a shallow well.

"Look how well off I am here!" he told a big turtle from the Eastern Ocean. "I can hop along the coping of the well when I go out, and rest by a crevice in the bricks on my return. I can wallow to my heart's content with only my head above water, or stroll ankle deep through soft mud. No crabs or tadpoles can compare with me. I am master of the water and lord of this shallow well. What more can a fellow ask? Why don't you come here more often to have a good time?"

Before the turtle from the Eastern Ocean could get his left foot into the well, however, he caught his right claw on something. So he halted and stepped back, then began to describe the ocean to the frog.

"It's more than a thousand *li* across and more than ten thousand feet deep. In ancient times there were floods nine years out of ten yet the water in the ocean never increased. And later there were droughts seven years out of eight yet the water in the ocean never grew less. It has remained quite constant throughout the ages. That is why I like to live in the Eastern Ocean."

Then the frog in the shallow well was silent and felt a little abashed.

埳井之蛙①

埳井之蛙……谓东海之鳖曰:"吾乐与!出跳梁乎井干之上,入休乎缺甃之崖②;赴水则接腋持颐③,蹶泥则没足灭跗④。还虷蟹与科斗⑤,莫吾能若也!且夫擅一壑之水,而跨跱埳井之乐⑥,此亦至矣。夫子奚不时来入观乎?"

东海之鳖,左足未入,而右膝已絷矣⑦。于是逡巡而却⑧,告之海,曰:"夫千里之远,不足以举其大;千仞之高,不足以极其深。禹之时,十年九潦⑨,而水弗为加益;汤之时,八年七旱,而崖不为加损。夫不为顷久推移,不以多少进退者,此亦东海之大乐也。"

于是埳井之蛙闻之,适适然惊⑩,规规然自失也⑪。

---

① 埳(kǎn 侃)井:浅井,坏井。
② 缺甃(zhòu 绉)之崖:残破的井壁。
③ 接腋持颐:青蛙入水时,水充两腋,面部则浮在水面。腋,胳肢窝。颐,下巴。
④ 蹶(jué 决):踏、踩。跗(fū 夫):脚背。
⑤ 还:回顾。虷(hán 寒):井中红色的虫子,俗称孑孓,蚊子的幼虫。
⑥ 跨跱(zhì 峙):叉开腿立着;屹立的样子。
⑦ 絷(zhí 执):绊住。
⑧ 逡(qūn 群)巡:欲进不进,迟疑不决。
⑨ 潦(lào 烙):同"涝"。雨水过多,淹没庄稼。
⑩ 适适然:惊讶恐惧的样子。
⑪ 规规然:渺小的样子。

英汉对照
English-Chinese
中国文学宝库
Gems of Chinese Literature
古代文学系列
Classical Literature

The Carp in the Dry Rut

When Zhuang Zi had no money, he went to the Lord Keeper of the River to borrow some grain.

"That's all right," said the lord. "I shall soon have collected the taxes from my fief; then I'll lend you three hundred gold pieces. How about that?"

Very indignant, Zhuang Zi told him this story:

As I was coming here yesterday I heard a voice calling me, and looking round I saw a carp lying in a dry rut on the road.

"How did you get there, carp?" I asked.

"I am a native of the Eastern Ocean," he replied. "Do you have a barrel of water to save my life?"

"That's all right," I told him. "I shall soon be visiting the princes of Wu and Yue in the south, and I shall let through some water for you from the West River. How about that?"

The carp was most indignant.

"I am out of my usual element," he said, "and don't know what to do. One barrel of water would save me, but you give me nothing but empty promises. You'll have to look for me later in the fish market."

辙中有鲋①

庄周家贫,故往贷粟于监河侯②。

监河侯曰:"诺!我将得邑金③,将贷子三百金,可乎?"

庄周忿然作色,曰:"周昨来,有中道而呼者④。周顾视车辙中,有鲋鱼焉。周问之曰:'鲋鱼,来!子何为者邪?'对曰:'我东海之波臣也⑤。君岂有斗升之水,而活我哉?'周曰:'诺!我且南游吴越之王⑥,激西江之水而迎子⑦,可乎?'鲋鱼忿然作色,曰:'吾失我常⑧,与我无所处;吾得斗升之水然活耳,君乃言此,曾不如早索我于枯鱼之肆⑨!'"

---

① 辙:车轮在泥地上辗出来的沟。鲋(fù付):鲫鱼。
② 贷粟:借粮。
③ 邑金:封邑的租税。
④ 中道:半路。呼:指呼救。
⑤ 波臣:波荡之臣,水族。
⑥ 游:指游说。
⑦ 激:激扬,把水从低处赶到高处。
⑧ 常:恒久不变叫常,指鱼的正常生活环境。
⑨ 肆:市集上的店铺。

英汉对照
English-Chinese
中国文学宝库
Gems of Chinese Literature
古代文学系列
Classical Literature

How Two Shepherd Boys Lost Their Sheep

Two shepherd boys, Gu and Zang, went out together with their flocks and both of them lost their sheep. When their master asked Zang what he had been doing, he answered that he had been reading. When Gu was questioned, he said he had been playing draughts.

They were doing different things, yet they both lost their sheep just the same.

臧谷亡羊

臧与谷二人①,相与牧羊,而俱亡其羊。
问臧奚事?则挟筴读书②;问谷奚事?则博塞以游③。
二人者事业不同,其于亡羊均也。

---

① 臧:男仆娶婢女所生的儿子称"臧"。谷:孺子,幼童。与"臧"同为奴隶的称谓。
② 筴:同"策",鞭子。
③ 博塞(sài 赛):古代的赌博游戏,如掷骰子之类。

Three Chestnuts or Four

A Monkey-trainer in the State of Song was fond of monkeys and kept a great many of them. He was able to understand them and they him. Indeed, he used to save some of his family's food for them. But a time came when there was not much food left at home, and he wanted to cut down the monkey's rations. He feared, however, they might not agree to this, and decided to deceive them.

"I'll give you three chestnuts each morning and four each evening," he said. "Will that be enough?"

All the monkeys rose up to express their anger.

"Well, what about four in the morning and three in the evening?" he asked.

Then the monkeys squatted down again, feeling quite satisfied.

狙公赋芧①

宋有狙公者,爱狙,养之成群。能解狙之意,狙亦得公之心。损其家口②,充狙之欲。

俄而匮焉③,将限其食。恐众狙之不驯于己也④,先诳之曰⑤:"与若芧⑥,朝三而暮四,足乎?"

众狙皆起而怒。

俄而曰:"与若芧,朝四而暮三,足乎?"

众狙皆伏而喜⑦。

---

① 狙(jū 居)公:好养猴子的人。狙,猕猴。
② 损其家口:指省下家人的口粮。
③ 匮(kuì 愧):贫困、不足。
④ 驯(xún 旬):顺服。
⑤ 诳(kuáng 狂):欺骗。
⑥ 芧(xù 序):橡树的果实,橡子。
⑦ 伏:同"匐",伏地。

英汉对照
English-Chinese
中国文学宝库
Gems of Chinese Literature
古代文学系列
Classical Literature

The Prince and His Bow

Prince Xuan was a keen archer and liked to be told what a powerful bowman he was, although he could draw no bow heavier than thirty catties. When he showed his bow to his attendants, they pretended to try to draw it, but merely bent it to half its full extent.

"This must weigh at least ninety catties!" they all cried. "None but Your Majesty could use such a bow."

And at this the prince was pleased.

Though he only used a thirty-catty bow, till the end of his life he believed that it weighed ninety catties. It was thirty in fact, and ninety merely in name; but for the sake of the empty name he sacrificed the truth.

宣王好射[①]

宣王好射,说人之谓己能用强也[②],其实所用不过三石[③]。以示左右,左右皆引试之[④],中关而止[⑤]。皆曰:"不下九石,非大王孰能用是[⑥]?"

宣王悦之。

然则宣王用不过三石,而终身自以为九石。三石,实也;九石,名也。宣王悦其名而丧其实。

---

① 宣王好射:齐宣王爱好射箭。
② 说:同"悦",喜欢。用强:指能拉开强硬的弓。
③ 石(dàn旦):重量的名称。古时三十斤为钧,四钧为石,即一百二十斤。但古时斤的分量要比现在轻。
④ 引:拉开弓。
⑤ 关(wān弯):同"弯"。中关,指拉弓刚到半弯的程度。
⑥ 孰能用是:谁能用此硬弓?

英汉对照
English-Chinese
中国文学宝库
Gems of Chinese Literature
古代文学系列
Classical Literature

Learning to Play Draughts

Playing draughts is a minor art; yet even so, you must give your whole attention to it to learn it. Qiu, the best draughts-player in the country, had two pupils. One of them concentrated entirely on what Qiu told them, while the other, though he also listened to his master, was thinking all the time of the wild geese in the sky, and itching to get his bow and arrows to shoot them. So he did not learn as well as the other pupil. It was not because he was less intelligent.

学 弈①

弈秋,通国之善弈者也②。
使弈秋诲二人弈③。其一人专心致志,惟弈秋之为听;一人虽听之,一心以为有鸿鹄将至④,思援弓缴而射之⑤。虽与之俱学,弗若之矣!
为是其智弗若与⑥?曰:非然也。

---

① 弈(yì 亦):围棋。
② 通国:全国。通,全、遍。
③ 诲:教导。
④ 鸿鹄(hú 斛):鹄也。即天鹅。
⑤ 缴(zhuó 灼):生丝,用以系在箭上。因称系着丝线的箭为"缴"。
⑥ 为:通"谓"。

英汉对照
English-Chinese
中国文学宝库
Gems of Chinese Literature
古代文学系列
Classical Literature

Helping Young Shoots to Grow

A man in the State of Song felt the shoots in his fields were not growing fast enough. So he pulled them all up, then went home quite exhausted.

"I'm tired out today," he told his family. "I've been helping the young shoots to grow."

His son ran out to the fields to have a look, and found all their seedlings were dead.

揠苗助长①

宋人有闵其苗之不长而揠之者②,芒芒然归③,谓其人曰④:"今日病矣⑤!予助苗长矣!"

其子趋而往视之,苗则槁矣⑥。

---

① 揠(yà 压)苗助长:拔苗助长。
② 闵:通"悯",忧虑。
③ 芒芒然:疲劳倦怠的样子。
④ 其人:指家里的人。
⑤ 病:疲倦,累坏。
⑥ 槁(gǎo 搞):枯干。

英汉对照
English-Chinese
中国文学宝库
Gems of Chinese Literature
古代文学系列
Classical Literature

The Man Who Was Afraid of Ghosts

There was once a man of southern Xia Shou by the name of Juan Shu Liang who was both slow-witted and cowardly.

Walking along a road one moonlit night, he saw his own shadow on the ground in front of him.

"It's a ghost crouching there!" he thought to himself.

Looking up, he saw a strand of hair dangling in front of his eyes.

"Oh! It's standing up now!" he thought.

He was so frightened he turned around and began to shuffle backwards.

As soon as he reached his home, he dropped to the ground, dead.

涓蜀梁

　　夏首之南有人焉①,曰涓蜀梁。其为人也,愚而善畏②。

　　明月而宵行,俯见其影,以为伏鬼也;卬视其发③,以为立魅也④。

　　背而走⑤,比至其家⑥,失气而死。

---

① 夏首:古地名,在今湖北省夏水之口。
② 善畏:胆子很小,容易害怕。
③ 卬:通"仰"。
④ 立魅(mèi 妹):站着的鬼怪。
⑤ 背而走:转身就跑。走,跑。
⑥ 比:及,等到。

The Man Who Was Found in the Well

The Ding family in the State of Song had no well of its own. Someone in the family sometimes had to spend a whole day doing nothing but fetch water from a distance.

To save trouble, they had a well sunk in their courtyard.

After the job was finished, they said to one another happily, "It seems with the sinking of the well one more person is added to our household."

One of Ding's friends heard of the remark and the word passed from that friend to that friend's friend and yet to another, until the story ran as follows: "The Dings had a well sunk and found a man inside!"

When the Duke of Song heard the tale he sent for Ding to inquire into the matter.

"With the sinking of the well it is as though your obedient servant has secured the help of a man," explained Ding to the Duke, "it isn't that I actually found a man in the well."

穿井得一人

宋之丁氏,家无井而出溉汲①,常一人居外。及其家穿井,告人曰:"吾穿井得一人。"

有闻而传之者曰:"丁氏穿井得一人。"国人道之,闻之于宋君。

宋君令人问之于丁氏,丁氏对曰:"得一人之使②,非得一人于井中也。"

---

① 溉汲:汲水浇地。
② 使:役,劳动力。

英汉对照
English-Chinese
中国文学宝库
Gems of Chinese Literature
古代文学系列
Classical Literature

The Son of a Good Swimmer

A Man walking along the river bank saw someone about to throw a small boy into the water. The child was screaming
"Why do you want to throw that child into the river?" asked the passer-by.
"His father is a good swimmer," was the answer.
But it does not follow that the son of a good swimmer can swim.

其父善游

有过于江上者,见人方引婴儿欲投之江中①,婴儿啼。

人问其故。

曰:"此其父善游。"

其父虽善游,其子岂遽善游哉②?

---

① 引:牵。
② 遽:遽然,突然,一下子。

Stealing the Bell

After the fall of the house of Fan, a man got hold of a bronze bell. It was too big to carry away on his back, and when he tried to break it with a hammer it made such a din that he feared others might hear and take it away from him. So he hastily stopped his ears.

It was all right to worry about others hearing the noise, but foolish to stop his own ears.

掩耳盗钟

范氏之亡也①,百姓有得钟者,欲负而走。则钟大不可负,以椎毁之,钟况然有音②。恐人闻之而夺己也,遽掩其耳③。

恶人闻之④,可也;恶己自闻之,悖矣⑤!

---

① 范氏之亡:指智伯伐范氏而灭之。范氏,晋卿范武子之后。
② 况然:形容钟声洪亮。
③ 遽:疾快。掩:掩盖、遮蔽、罩住。
④ 恶(wù 误):憎恨,讨厌,害怕。
⑤ 悖(bèi 背):荒谬。

英汉对照
English-Chinese
中国文学宝库
Gems of Chinese Literature
古代文学系列
Classical Literature

Painting Ghosts

There was an artist who worked for the prince of Qi.

"Tell me," said the prince, "what are the hardest things to paint?"

"Dogs, horses, and the like," replied the artist.

"What are the easiest?" asked the prince.

"Ghosts and monsters," the artist told him. "We all know dogs and horses and see them every day; but it is hard to make an exact likeness of them. That is why they are difficult subjects. But ghosts and monsters have no definite form, and no one has ever seen them; so they are easy to paint."

说　画

客有为齐王画者。齐王问曰:"画孰最难者?"

曰:"犬马最难。"

"孰易者?"

曰:"鬼魅最易①。"

夫犬马,人所知也,旦暮罄于前②,不可类之③,故难;鬼魅无形者,不罄于前,故易之也。

---

① 鬼魅(mèi 妹):鬼怪。魅,世俗迷信以为物老便成魅。
② 罄(qìng 庆):显现。
③ 类:相似。

The Crumbling Wall

There was once a rich man in the State of Song. After a downpour of rain his wall began to crumble.

"If you don't mend that wall," warned his son, "a thief will get in."

An old neighbour gave the same advice.

That night, indeed, a great deal of money was stolen. Then the rich man commended his son's intelligence, but suspected his old neighbour of being the thief.

宋有富人

　　宋有富人①,天雨墙坏。其子曰:"不筑,必将有盗。"其邻人之父亦云。
　　暮而果大亡其财②。
　　其家皆智其子,而疑邻人之父。

---

①　宋:同书《说林下》作"郑"。
②　亡:失、被盗。

Ivory Chopsticks

When King Zhou ordered chopsticks made of ivory, Ji Zi was most perturbed. For he feared that once the king had ivory chopsticks he would not be content with earthenware, but would want cups of rhinoceros horn and jade; and instead of beans and vegetables, he would insist on such delicacies as elephant's tail and baby leopard. He would hardly be willing either to wear rough homespun or live under a thatched roof, but would demand silks and splendid mansions.

"It is fear of what this will lead to," said Ji Zi, "that upsets me."

Five years later, indeed, King Zhou had a garden filled with meat, tortured his subjects with hot irons, and caroused in a lake of wine. And so he lost his kingdom.

纣为象箸

昔者,纣为象箸而箕子怖①。以为象箸必不加于土铏②,必将犀玉之杯;象箸、玉杯,必不羹菽藿③,则必旄、象、豹胎④;旄、象、豹胎,必不衣短褐而食于茅屋之下⑤,则必锦衣九重,广室高台。"吾畏其卒,故怖其始。"

居五年,纣为肉圃⑥,设炮烙⑦,登糟丘⑧,临酒池,纣遂以亡。

---

① 象箸:象牙筷子。箕子:殷之太师,谏纣王被囚,佯狂为奴。
② 土铏:泥土制作的器皿。
③ 羹菽藿(gēng shū huò 庚叔霍):大豆汤之类。羹,汤;菽,豆类总名;藿,豆叶。
④ 旄(máo 毛):旄牛。
⑤ 短褐:穷人穿的半截麻布袄。
⑥ 肉圃:肉林。
⑦ 炮烙:烙,当作"格",指铜格。其下生火,取生肉置格上,炮而食之。又纣王曾以炮烙作刑具,残杀敢于反抗他的人。
⑧ 糟丘:积酒糟成山丘。

英汉对照
English-Chinese
中国文学宝库
Gems of Chinese Literature
古代文学系列
Classical Literature

The Man Who Pretended He Could Play Reed Pipes

When Prince Xuan of Qi called for reed pipe music, he would have three hundred men playing at the same time. Then a scholar named Nanguo asked for a place in the orchestra, and the prince, taking a fancy to him, gave him a salary large enough to feed several hundred men.

After Prince Xuan's death, Prince Min came to the throne, and he liked solo performance.

There upon the scholar fled.

滥竽充数

齐宣王使人吹竽①,必三百人。

南郭处士②请为王吹竽,宣王说之,廪食以数百人③。

宣王死,湣王立,好一一听之,处士逃。

---

① 竽:古代簧管乐器名,三十六簧。形似笙而略大。
② 处士:古时称有学行而没有做官的人为"处士"。这个南郭处士却是个没有真才实学,冒充内行,混水摸鱼,骗取名利的人。
③ 廪(lǐn 懔)食:由公家供给粮食。以数百人:吹竽之人由官廪供食者已近数百人。

英汉对照
English-Chinese
中国文学宝库
Gems of Chinese Literature
古代文学系列
Classical Literature

The Man Who Sold Spears and Shields

In the State of Chu lived a man who sold shields and spears.

"My shields are so strong," he boasted, "that nothing can pierce them. My spears are so sharp there is nothing they cannot pierce."

"What if one of your spears strikes one of your shields?" someone asked him.

The man had no answer to that.

矛　盾①

人有鬻矛与楯者②,誉其楯之坚:"物莫能陷也③。"俄而又誉其矛,曰:"吾矛之利,物无不陷也。"

人应之曰:"以子之矛,陷子之楯,何如?"其人弗能应也。

以为不可陷之楯与无不陷之矛,为名不可两立也④。

---

① 矛:古时长柄有刃的兵器,用以刺敌。盾:古代武器名,即藤牌或皮牌,用以抵挡敌人刀箭,防护身体。
② 楯(dùn 顿):同"盾"。
③ 陷:深入,穿破。
④ 名:指事物之理。

英汉对照
English-Chinese
中国文学宝库
Gems of Chinese Literature
古代文学系列
Classical Literature

A Recipe for Immortality

A stranger informed the Prince of Yan that he could make him immortal, and the prince bade one of his subjects learn this art; but before the man could do so the stranger died. Then the prince, in great anger, executed his subject.

He failed to see that the stranger was cheating him, but taken in by his lies had an innocent citizen killed. This shows what a fool he was! For a man values nothing more than his own life, yet this fellow could not even keep himself alive, so what could he do for the prince?

燕王学道

客有教燕王为不死之道者①,王使人学之,所使学者未及学而客死。

王大怒,诛之。王不知客之欺己,而诛学者之晚也②。

夫信不然之物而诛无罪之臣③,不察之患也。且人所急无如其身,不能自使其无死,安能使王长生哉?

---

① 燕:战国时诸侯国之一。不死之道:指长生不老之术。
② 晚:指去学习迟了。
③ 不然之物:指根本不会有的事情。

How Two Water Snakes Moved House

The snakes wanted to move away from a marsh which was drying up.

"If you lead the way and I follow," said a small to a large snake, "men will know we are moving away and someone will kill you. You had better carry me on your back, each holding the other's tail in his mouth. Then men will think I am a god."

So, each holding the other, they crossed the highway. And everybody made way for them, crying out: "This is a god!"

涸泽之蛇

泽涸①,蛇将徙②。

有小蛇谓大蛇曰:"子行而我随之,人以为蛇之行者耳,必有杀子者;子不如相衔负我以行③,人必以我为神君也。"

乃相衔负,以越公道而行。人皆避之曰:"神君也!"

---

① 泽:池塘、湖沼。涸(hé 河):干枯。
② 徙(xǐ 喜):迁移。
③ 衔负:背负。

Selling the Casket Without the Pearls

A native of the State of Chu decided to sell some pearls in the State of Zheng. He had a casket made of rare wood, scented it with spices, inlaid it with jade and other precious jewels, and wrapped it in kingfishers' plumage. The result was that the men of Zheng were eager to buy the casket, but he could not sell his pearls.

This fellow may be considered a skilled casket seller, but deserves no credit at all as a seller of pearls.

买椟还珠

楚人有卖其珠于郑者,为木兰之柜①,熏以桂椒②,缀以珠玉,饰以玫瑰③,辑以羽翠④。郑人买其椟而还其珠。

此可谓善卖椟矣,未可谓善鬻珠也⑤。

---

① 木兰:又名杜兰、林兰或木莲。木肌细而心黄,质料坚固美观。柜:这里指匣子。
② 桂椒:指牡桂和花椒,都是香料名。
③ 玫瑰:美石。
④ 辑:通"缉"。羽翠:即翡翠。
⑤ 鬻(yù浴):卖。

The Rumour About Zeng Shen

Once, when Zeng Shen went to the district of Fei, a man with the same name there committed a murder. Someone went to tell Zeng Shen's mother: "Zeng Shen has killed a man!"

"Impossible," she replied. "My son would never do such a thing."

She went calmly on with her weaving.

After a while, someone else came to report: "Zeng Shen has killed a man."

Still the old lady went on weaving.

Then a third man came to tell her: "Zeng Shen has killed a man!"

This time his mother was frightened. She threw down her shuttle and escaped over the wall.

曾母投杼[1]

昔者曾子处费[2]。

费人有与曾子同名族者[3],而杀人。人告曾子母曰:"曾参杀人!"曾子之母曰:"吾子不杀人。"织自若[4]。

有顷焉,人又曰:"曾参杀人!"其母尚织自若也。

顷之,一人又告曰:"曾参杀人!"其母惧,投杼逾墙而走。

---

[1] 杼(zhù 柱):织布梭子。
[2] 费(mì 秘):地名,鲁邑。旧城在今山东省费县西南。
[3] 同名族:同名同姓的人。
[4] 织自若:只管织自己的布。若,如故。

英汉对照
English-Chinese
中国文学宝库
Gems of Chinese Literature
古代文学系列
Classical Literature

The Wrong Direction

The Prince of Wei decided to invade Handan, the capital of the State of Zhao. Although Jiliang was on a journey when he heard this, he turned back at once and, without waiting to smooth his crumpled garments or brush the dust from his head, went to see the king.

"On my way back," he said, "I came across a man at Taihang Mountain, who was riding northwards. He told me he was going to the State of Chu.

" 'In that case, why are you heading north?' I asked him.

" 'That's all right,' he replied. 'I have good horses.'

" 'Your horses may be good, but you're taking the wrong direction.'

" 'Well, I have plenty of money.'

" 'You may have plenty of money, but this is the wrong direction.'

" 'Well, I have an excellent charioteer.'

" 'The better your horses', I told him, 'the more money you have and the more skilled your charioteer, the further you will get from the State of Chu.'"

南辕北辙①

魏王欲攻邯郸②,季梁闻之③,中道而反,衣焦不申④,头尘不去⑤,往见王,曰:"今者,臣来,见人于大行⑥,方北面而持其驾⑦,告臣曰:'我欲之楚'。臣曰:'君之楚,将奚为北面?'曰:'吾马良!'臣曰:'马虽良,此非楚之路也。'曰:'吾用多⑧。'臣曰:'用虽多,此非楚路也。'曰:'吾御者善。'——此数者愈善,而离楚愈远耳!"

---

① 南辕北辙:车辕向南而车辙向北。比喻背道而驰、行动和目的相反。辕,车前驾车的车杠;辙,车轮行过留下的印迹。
② 魏王:即安釐王圉。邯郸:赵国国都,在今河北邯郸市。
③ 季梁:魏国贤人。
④ 衣焦:衣服褶绉。申:同"伸",伸展。
⑤ 去:一本作"浴"。
⑥ 大行:大路。一说指太行山。
⑦ 持其驾:手持缰绳驾着车。
⑧ 用:资用,指路费。

英汉对照
English-Chinese
中国文学宝库
Gems of Chinese Literature
古代文学系列
Classical Literature

Drawing a Snake with Legs

In the State of Chu, a man who had held a sacrifice gave the goblet of sacrificial wine to his stewards.

"This is not enough for us all," said the stewards, "but more than enough for one. Let's draw snakes on the ground, and the one who finishes first can have the wine."

The man who finished first picked up the goblet, but holding it in his left hand went on drawing with his right.

"I am adding some legs," he said.

Before he finished the legs, though, another steward completed his drawing and took the goblet from him.

"A snake has no legs," said this last. "Why should you add legs?"

So he drained the wine instead. And the one who had drawn the legs had nothing to drink.

画蛇添足

楚有祠者①,赐其舍人卮酒②。

舍人相谓曰:"数人饮之不足,一人饮之有余。请画地为蛇,先成者饮酒。"

一人蛇先成,引酒且饮,乃左手持卮③,右手画蛇曰:"吾能为之足!"

未成,一人之蛇成,夺其卮,曰:"蛇固无足,子安能为之足?"遂饮其酒。

为蛇足者,终亡其酒。

---

① 祠:春祭。
② 舍人:战国时候,王公贵族都有舍人,即门客。
③ 卮(zhī 支):古时盛酒的器具。

英汉对照
English-Chinese
中国文学宝库
Gems of Chinese Literature
古代文学系列
Classical Literature

Buying a Good Horse

There was a king who was willing to pay a thousand pieces of gold for a horse that could run a thousand *li* without stopping. For three years he tried in vain to find such a steed.

Then someone offered: "Let me look for a horse for Your Majesty."

The king agreed to this.

After three months this man came back, having spent five hundred pieces of gold on a horse's skull.

The king was most enraged.

"I want a live horse!" he roared. "What use is a dead horse to me? Why spend five hundred pieces of gold on nothing?"

But the man replied: "If you will spend five hundred pieces of gold on a dead horse, won't you give much more for a live one? When people hear of this, they will know you are really willing to pay for a good horse, and will quickly send you their best."

Sure enough, in less than a year the king succeeded in buying three excellent horses.

千金买首

古之君人①,有以千金求千里马者,三年不能得。

涓人言于君曰②:"请求之。"

君遣之。三月得千里马,马已死,买其首五百金,反以报君。

君大怒曰:"所求者生马,安事死马③?而捐五百金!"

涓人对曰:"死马且买之五百金,况生马乎?天下必以王为能市马④,马今至矣。"

于是不能期年⑤,千里之马至者三。

---

① 君人:即人君。
② 涓(juān 娟)人:国君的近侍。即中涓,官名,俗称太监。
③ 安事:犹言"何用"。
④ 市马:买马。
⑤ 期年:一整年。

英汉对照
English-Chinese
中国文学宝库
Gems of Chinese Literature
古代文学系列
Classical Literature

Who Deserved the Place of Honour

A man passing a friend's house noticed that the kitchen chimney was straight, and a pile of fuel was stacked beside the stove.

"You had better build another chimney with a bend in it," he advised the householder. "And move that fuel away, otherwise it may catch fire."

But the master of the house ignored his advice.

Later the house did catch fire; but luckily the neighbours came and helped to put it out. Then that family killed an ox and prepared wine to express their thanks to the neighbours. Those who had received burns were seated in the places of honour, and the rest according to their merit; but no mention was made of the man who had advised them to build a new chimney.

"If you had taken that man's advice," someone said to the master of the house, "you could have saved the expense of the ox and wine, and avoided a fire. Now you are entertaining your friends to thank them for what they did. But is it right to ignore the man who advised you to rebuild the chimney and move the firewood, while you treat those who received burns as guests of honour?"

Then the master of the house realized his mistake, and invited the man who had given him good advice.

曲突徙薪①

客有过主人者②,见灶直突,傍有积薪③。

客谓主人曰:"曲其突,远其积薪。不者,将有火患。"

主人默然不应。

居无几何,家果失火。乡聚里中人哀而救之④,火幸息⑤。

于是杀牛置酒,燔发灼烂者在上行⑥,余各用功次坐⑦,而反不录言曲突者⑧。向使主人听客之言,不费牛酒,终无火患。

---

① 曲突徙薪:把烟囱改建成弯的,搬开灶旁的柴,避免发生火灾。曲,使之弯曲;突,烟囱;徙,迁移;薪,柴。
② 过:探望、拜访。
③ 傍:临近、旁边。
④ 乡:古制一万二千五百家为一乡。聚:村落。里:古制五家为邻,五邻为里,即二十五家为里。另有五十户、一百户等说。乡聚里中人,即指乡里的邻居们。
⑤ 息:同"熄",熄灭。
⑥ 燔(fán 凡):焚烧。灼(zhuó 酌):炙、烧。上行(háng 杭):上席。
⑦ 用:以、按。次坐:依次安排座位。
⑧ 录:采纳。延请之意。

英汉对照
English-Chinese
中国文学宝库
Gems of Chinese Literature
古代文学系列
Classical Literature

Playing the Harp to an Ox

One day Gong Mingyi, the celebrated musician, was playing an elegant tune on his harp to amuse a browsing ox.

The ox, however, continued to munch, paying no heed to him at all.

Then he struck up some different notes, which sounded like mosquitoes droning and calves bleating. Whereupon the ox flicked its tail, pricked up its ears, and began frisking round and round, evidently absorbed in the music.

对牛弹琴

昔公明仪为牛弹清角之操①,伏食如故。非牛不闻,不合其耳矣。

转为蚊虻之声②、孤犊之鸣③,即掉尾奋耳,蹀躞而听④。

---

① 公明仪:人名。清角:古曲调名,声音清淡高雅。角,为中国五声(宫、商、角、徵、羽)之一。《管子》云:"凡听角,如雉登木以鸣,音疾以清。"操:琴曲。

② 蚊虻(méng 萌):蚊子和牛虻。虻,昆虫名,即牛虻,似蝇稍大,雌虫刺吸牛畜等的血液,有时也吸人血。

③ 孤犊(dú 毒):离群的小牛。

④ 蹀躞(dié xiè 蝶谢):小步走路的样子。蹀,蹈足。

英汉对照
English-Chinese
中国文学宝库
Gems of Chinese Literature
古代文学系列
Classical Literature

Lamenting a Mother's Death

The mother of a man living in the east of a village died, and he lamented her death; but he did not sound too sad. When the son of a woman living in the west of the village saw this, he went home and said to his mother: "Why don't you hurry up and die? I promise to lament you very bitterly."

A man who looks forward to his mother's death will hardly be able to lament it bitterly.

哭母不哀

东家母死,其子哭之不哀。

西家子见之,归谓其母曰:"社何爱速死①?吾必悲哭社!"

夫欲其母之死者,虽死亦不能悲哭矣。

---

① 社:古代江、淮一带方言称母为"社"。

A Scholar Buys a Donkey

One day a learned scholar was buying a donkey on the market.

A deed had to be filled out recording the transaction.

He wrote sheet after sheet till three sheets were finished, but still the word "donkey" did not appear on the paper.

If you learn from such a scholar, you'll follow the way of the donkey.

博士买驴

博士买驴①,书券三纸②,未有驴字。使汝以此为师,令人气塞③。

---

① 博士:古官名,历代职司不同,一般掌通古今史事待问及书籍典守。间亦参预政事讨论,或仅掌礼仪而已。
② 书券:书籍。古时书本作卷轴形,故称"书券"。纸:指书的件数或张数。
③ 气塞:呼吸堵塞不通。

英汉对照
English-Chinese
中国文学宝库
Gems of Chinese Literature
古代文学系列
Classical Literature

The Man Who Liked Money Better Than Life

In Yongzhou there were many good swimmers. One day, the river swelled suddenly. Braving the danger, about half a dozen people started across in a small boat. While they were still in midstream, the boat capsized. Whereupon, they started to swim. One, though using his arms vigorously, seemed to make small progress.

"You're a better swimmer than any of us, why are you lagging behind?" asked his companions.

"I have a thousand coins tied around my loin," said the man.

"Why don't you throw them away?" urged the others.

He made no answer, shaking his head, although he was clearly in difficulties.

The others reached the shore and shouted out to him: "Off with the coins, you fool! What's the use of the money to you when you are drowning?"

Still the man shook his head. In a few moments he was drowned.

溺者之死货①

永之氓咸善游②。一日,水暴甚,有五六氓,乘小船绝湘水③。中济,船破,皆游④,其一氓尽力而不能寻常⑤。

其侣曰:"汝善游最也,今何后为?"

曰:"吾腰千钱,重,是以后。"

曰:"何不去之?"

不应,摇其首。有顷,益怠。

已济者立岸上,呼且号曰:"汝愚之甚!蔽之甚⑥!身且死,何以货为?"

又摇其首,遂溺死。

---

① 溺者之死货:这里只截录《哀溺文》序的一段,取《哀溺文》首句"吾哀溺者之死货兮"词意为题。
② 永:即永州,今湖南省零陵县。氓:平民。咸:都。
③ 绝:穿过、越过、横渡。湘水:即今湖南省湘江。
④ "皆游":一作"皆浮游"。
⑤ 寻常:八尺为"寻",倍寻为"常",这里指游得很慢。
⑥ 蔽:蒙蔽、不聪明、糊涂。

英汉对照
English-Chinese
中国文学宝库
Gems of Chinese Literature
古代文学系列
Classical Literature

The Donkey of Guizhou

There were no donkeys in Guizhou until an eccentric took one there by boat; but finding no use for it he set it loose in the hills. A tiger who saw this monstrous-looking beast thought it must be divine. It first surveyed the donkey from under cover, then ventured a little nearer, still keeping a respectful distance however.

One day the donkey brayed, and the tiger took fright and fled, for fear of being bitten. It was utterly terrified. But it came back for another look, and decided this creature was not so formidable after all. Then, growing used to the braying, it drew nearer, though it still dared not attack. Coming nearer still, it began to take liberties, shoving, jostling, and charging roughly, till the donkey lost its temper and kicked out.

"So that is all it can do!" thought the tiger, greatly pleased.

Then it leaped on the donkey and sank its teeth into it, severing its throat and devouring it before going on its way.

黔之驴①

黔无驴,有好事者船载以入。至,则无可用,放之山下。

虎见之,庞然大物也,以为神。蔽林间窥之,稍出,近之,慭慭然莫相知②。

他日,驴一鸣,虎大骇,远遁,以为且噬己也③,甚恐。然往来视之,觉无异能者,益习其声。又近出前后,终不敢搏④。稍近,益狎,荡倚冲冒⑤。驴不胜怒⑥,蹄之。虎因喜,计之曰:"技止此耳!"因跳踉大㘎⑦,断其喉,尽其肉,乃去。

---

① 黔(qián 虔)之驴:贵州的驴子。黔,今贵州省的别名。唐朝时设黔中道,辖今四川省南部和贵州省北部地区。
② 慭(yìn 印)慭然:恭敬谨慎的样子。
③ 噬(shì 是):咬、吃。
④ 搏:捕捉。
⑤ 荡:摇动、摆摇。倚:靠近。冲冒:冲撞冒犯。
⑥ 不胜(shēng 生):不禁。
⑦ 跳踉(láng 郎,又读 liáng 良):腾跃跳动。㘎(hǎn 喊):老虎怒吼的样子。

131

The Silly Fawn

A man in Linjiang captured a fawn. When it was brought home, the dogs came licking their chops and wagging their tails. The man angrily drove them off. Afterwards, he took the fawn among the dogs, warning them to keep their peace, and making them frolic with it. In time, the dogs learned their lesson. As the fawn grew, it forgot it was a deer and regarded the dogs as its friends, with whom it could gambol and play. The dogs, fearing their master, had to suppress their natural desires and fraternize with it.

One day after three years, the deer went outside the gate. There were many strange dogs in the street, so it went up and tried to play with them. The dogs were surprised, but being glad to see a meal come their way, fell upon it and killed it. As it was breathing its last, the deer was at a loss to understand why it had come to such an untimely end.

临江之麋①

临江之人,畋得麋麑②,畜之。入门,群犬垂涎,扬尾皆来。其人怒,怛之③。自是日抱就犬④,习示之⑤,使勿动,稍使与之戏。

积久,犬皆如人意。麋麑稍大,忘己之麋也,以为犬良我友⑥,抵触偃仆⑦,益狎⑧。犬畏主人,与之俯仰甚善,然时啖其舌⑨。

三年,麋出门,见外犬在道甚众,走欲与为戏。外犬见而喜,且怒,共杀食之,狼藉道上⑩。麋至死不悟。

---

① 临江:今江西省清江县。麋(mí迷):即麋鹿。
② 畋(tián 田):打猎。麋麑(ní泥):鹿的幼儿。
③ 怛(dá 达):恐吓、惊吓。
④ 就:趋从、凑近。
⑤ 习:常。
⑥ 良:的确、良是。
⑦ 抵触:相互碰撞。偃(yǎn 演)仆:仰卧扑倒。指上下翻滚、戏耍打闹的样子。
⑧ 益:愈加。狎(xiá 侠):亲昵。
⑨ 啖(dàn 但):吃,这里指"舔",表示贪馋的样子。
⑩ 狼藉(jí即):纵横凌乱的样子。旧传狼群时藉草而卧,起身时则践草使乱以灭其踪迹,后因称"狼藉"为散乱的形容词。

英汉对照
English-Chinese
中国文学宝库
Gems of Chinese Literature
古代文学系列
Classical Literature

Ancient Books for Ancient Bronze

A scholar, hard-pressed for money, listed a few hundred of his books, packed them up, and set out for the capital, intending to sell them. On his way he met another scholar who looked at his list and wanted to buy them. But he could not afford the price. He happened to have a few pieces of ancient bronze at home which he intended to sell for rice. So he took the other to see them. The one who wanted to sell his books was a great admirer of bronze, and was delighted with these specimens.

"No need to sell them," he told the other. "We can weigh the price of the books against the bronze and see if we can't do an exchange." The outcome was that he deposited his books with the other and left with a load of bronze.

When he reached home, his wife was surpised to see him back so soon. Looking quickly at his bags, she found they were full of some hard objects which clanged when shifted about. When she heard the story, she began to scold.

"You fool!" she exclaimed. "What do you want these things for when we have no rice in the house?"

"He's in the same fix," replied the husband, cheerfully. "With the books he has from me, he won't have any rice to eat for some time either!"

古书换古器

有一士人,尽掊其家所有①,约百余千,买书,将以入京②。至中涂,遇一士人,取其书目阅之,爱其书而贫不能得,家有数古铜器将以货之③。而鬻书者雅有好古器之癖④,一见喜甚。乃曰:"无庸货也⑤,我将与汝估其直而两易之⑥。"

于是,尽以随行之书换数十铜器。

亟返其家⑦,其妻方讶夫之回,疾视其行李,但见二三布囊磊磈然⑧,铿铿有声⑨。问得其实,乃詈其夫曰⑩:"你换得他这个,几时近得饭吃⑪?"

其人曰:"他换得我那个也,则几时近得饭吃?"

---

① 掊(pǒu 剖):破、折。
② 将:拿。
③ 货:出卖。
④ 鬻(yù 育):卖。雅:特别。癖:积久成习的嗜好。
⑤ 无庸:不必。
⑥ 直:同"值",价值。易:交换。
⑦ 亟:紧、急切。
⑧ 磊磈(kuǐ 傀)然:众石块高低不平的样子。
⑨ 铿(kēng 坑)铿:象声词,叮叮当当的撞击声。
⑩ 詈(lì 利):责骂。
⑪ 近:接近、求得。

英汉对照
English-Chinese
中国文学宝库
Gems of Chinese Literature
古代文学系列
Classical Literature

The Boat-Owner's Bright Idea

Once I saw a man travelling on foot at Lüliang. He saw a boat, and offered the boat-owner fifty coins to take him to Pengmen.

"According to the usual rates," said the boat-owner, "a passenger making a trip without cargo should pay a hundred coins. Now you're offering half, that't not enough. But since I have to pay fifty coins for a man to tow my boat, I'll take you for fifty if you agree to tow my boat to Pengmen!"

可折半直①

艾子见有人徒行,自吕梁托舟人以趋彭门者②,持五十钱遗舟师③。

师曰:"凡无赍而独载者人百金④。汝尚少半,汝当自此为我挽牵至彭门⑤,可折半直也。"

---

① 折:折合、抵作。半直:一半的价钱。直,通"值",价值。
② 吕梁:山名,此指江苏省铜山县东南之吕梁,其下亦称吕梁洪。彭门:当指彭城,县名,古大彭氏之地,即今江苏省铜山县治。趋:向、往。
③ 遗(wèi 位):送给。舟师:撑船的师傅。
④ 赍(jī 机):旅行人携带的行李、衣食等物。
⑤ 挽牵:拉着船纤。牵,同"纤"。

英汉对照
English-Chinese
中国文学宝库
Gems of Chinese Literature
古代文学系列
Classical Literature

What Does the Sun Look Like?

A man who was born blind wanted to know what the sun looked like, so he asked others to describe it.

"It looks like this, like a bronze disc," said one, rapping a gong as he spoke. Some time later, when the blind man heard a gong, he said, "Isn't that the sun?"

Another told him, "The sun has light like this candle," and let him feel the candle. Some time later, the blind man picked up a flute and exclaimed, "Ah! This is surely the sun."

A sun is a far cry from a gong or a flute, but the blind cannot make out the difference because they cannot see and have to ask others.

日　喻

生而眇者不识日①,问之有目者。

或告之曰:"日之状如铜盘。"

扣盘而得其声。他日闻钟,以为日也。

或告之曰:"日之光如烛。"

扪烛而得其形②。他日揣籥③,以为日也。

日之与钟、籥亦远矣,而眇者不知其异,以其未尝见而求之人也。

---

① 眇(miǎo 秒)者:这里指瞎眼的人。眇,原指一只眼瞎,见《易·履》云:"眇能视。"
② 扪(mén 门):抚摸。
③ 揣:量度,揣度。籥(yuè 跃):古代管乐器,似笛而短。籥,本字作"龠",见甲骨文,像编管之形,当为"排箫"之前身。这里用作单管的竹制乐器。

英汉对照
English-Chinese
中国文学宝库
Gems of Chinese Literature
古代文学系列
Classical Literature

The Fighting Oxen

An art lover collected hundreds of paintings and calligraphic works, and the one he loved best was a picture of fighting oxen done by Dai Song. He had the painting mounted on precious silk hung from jade rods, and hid it away in a cedar chest.

One day he took the painting from the chest, unrolled it, and hung it in the sun, as a precaution against bookworms.

Just then a cowherd entered the courtyard. At sight of the painting of fighting oxen the boy laughed.

"When oxen fight and butt with their horns," said the boy, "they keep their tails tucked between their rumps. But in this picture, they're flicking their tails about. Isn't this ridiculous?"

The art collector had to smile and agree with him.

戴嵩画牛①

蜀中有杜处士,好书画,所宝以百数。有戴嵩牛一轴,尤所爱,锦囊玉轴,常以自随。一日曝书画②,有一牧童见之,拊掌大笑③。曰:"此画斗牛也。斗牛力在角,尾搐入两股间④。今乃掉尾而斗⑤,谬矣!"处士笑而然之。

---

① 戴嵩:唐朝著名画家,善画水牛。
② 曝(pù 铺):晒。
③ 拊(fǔ 府)掌:拍手。
④ 搐(chù 触):抽缩。
⑤ 掉尾:摇尾。

英汉对照
English-Chinese
中国文学宝库
Gems of Chinese Literature
古代文学系列
Classical Literature

Treating Hunchbacks

There was once a charlatan who claimed he could cure deformities of the spine. "Whether your back is like a bow, a shrimp, a ring, or whatever you please, come to me and I'll straighten it in no time."

One hunchback was credulous enough to take his words at their face value and came to him for treatment. The charlatan made him lie prone on a plank, put another on his hump, then jumped up and down on it with all his might. The hump was straightened, but the man died.

The man's son wanted to sue him, but the charlatan said, "My job is to straighten his hump. Whether or not he dies has nothing to do with me."

驼 医

昔有医人,自媒能治背驼①,曰:"如弓者,如虾者,如曲环者,延吾治,可朝治而夕如矢。"

一人信焉,而使治驼。

乃索板二片,以一置地下,卧驼者其上,又以一压焉,而即蹁焉②,驼者随直,亦复随死。其子欲鸣诸官,医人曰:"我业治驼,但管人直,那管人死!"

① 自媒:自我介绍、自我吹嘘。
② 蹁(xǐ):踏。

The Dream

There was once a proctor who was very strict with his students. One day, a student committed a breach of discipline. Pulling a long face, the proctor sent for the offender, and sat himself in a chair to await his arrival. The student finally appeared, and, kneeling before the proctor, said, "I meant to come earlier. But the fact is I have just found a thousand ounces of gold and I've had a hard time deciding how to dispose of it."

The proctor melted a little when he heard about the gold. "Where did you find it?" he asked.

"Buried under the ground!"

"And what are you going to do with it?" asked the proctor again.

"I was a poor man, sir," answered the student. "I have talked it over with my wife and we agreed to put aside 500 ounces to buy land, 200 for a house, 100 to buy furniture and another hundred to buy maidservants and pages. Then we'll use one half of the last hundred to buy books, for from now on I must study hard, and the other half I will make as a small present to you for the pains you took in educating me."

狡生梦金

尝闻一青衿①,生性狡,能以谲计诳人②。

其学博持教甚严③,诸生稍或犯规,必遣人执之,扑无赦④。

一日,此生适有犯。学博追执甚急,坐彝伦堂盛怒待之⑤。已而生至,长跪地下,不言他事,但曰:"弟子偶得千金,方在处置,故来见迟耳!"

博士闻生得金多,辄霁怒⑥,问之曰:"尔金从何处来?"

曰:"得诸地中。"

又问:"尔欲作何处置?"

生答曰:"弟子故贫,无资业,今与妻计:以五百金市田,二百金市宅,百金置器具、买童妾。止剩百金,以其半市书,将发愤从事焉,而以其半致馈先生⑦,酬平日教育,完矣。"

---

① 青衿(jīn 今):古时学子所穿的青领服装。这里指学生。衿,同"襟",古代衣服的交领。
② 谲(jué 决)计:欺诈的计策。
③ 学博:学识广博的人,这里指学堂教师。下文的"博士",亦指此。
④ 扑:古时教师的教刑(杖)。这里用作动词。
⑤ 彝伦堂:堂屋的匾额名。彝伦,即伦常,旧指人与人之间的道德关系。
⑥ 霁怒:比喻怒气消散。
⑦ 致馈(kuì 溃):敬送。馈,泛指赠送。

英汉对照
English-Chinese
中国文学宝库
Gems of Chinese Literature
古代文学系列
Classical Literature

The Dream

"Ah! Is that so! I don't think I have done enough to deserve so precious a gift," said the proctor.

So saying, he ordered his cook to prepare a sumptuous dinner to which he invited the student. They had a happy time, talking and laughing and toasting each other's health. Just as they were getting tipsy, the proctor had a sudden thought.

"You came away in a hurry," he said. "Did you remember to lock the gold away in a cabinet before you came?"

The student rose to his feet. "Sir, I had just finished planning how to use the money when my wife rolled against me, and I opened my eyes to find the gold was gone. So what's the use of the cabinet?"

"So all this you've been talking about is only a dream?" gasped the proctor.

"Indeed, yes," answered the student.

The proctor was angry, but since he had been so hospitable to the student, it would have seemed churlish to lose his temper with him now, so he contented himself with saying, "I can see you keep me in mind even when you are dreaming. Surely you won't forget me when you really have the gold?"

And he urged him to more drinks before he let him go.

博士曰："有是哉！不佞何以当之①？"遂呼使者治具，甚丰洁，延生坐觞之②，谈笑欵洽，皆异平日。饮半酣，博士问生曰："尔适匆匆来，亦曾收金箧中扃钥耶③？"

生起应曰："弟子布置此金甫定④，为荆妻转身触弟子，醒已失金所在，安用箧！"

博士蘧然曰⑤："尔所言金，梦耶？"

生答曰："固梦耳！"

博士不怿⑥，然业与欵洽，不能复怒，徐曰："尔自雅情⑦，梦中得金，犹不忘先生，况实得耶！"更一再觞出之。

---

① 不佞：犹不才，用作自称的谦词。
② 觞(shāng 伤)：向人敬酒。
③ 箧(qiè 怯)：小匣子。扃钥：关闭加锁。扃，门窗箱柜上的插关，引申为关锁。
④ 甫：刚才、开始。
⑤ 蘧(qú 渠)然：惊讶的样子。
⑥ 怿(yì 译)：喜悦。
⑦ 雅情：高尚的感情。

英汉对照
English-Chinese
中国文学宝库
Gems of Chinese Literature
古代文学系列
Classical Literature

Nothing to Do with Me

A surgeon once boasted about his ability. A soldier, returning from battle with an arrow penetrating his leg, came to him for treatment.

The surgeon took a pair of sharp scissors and cut off the stem of the arrow close to the flesh, then asked for pay.

"But you haven't taken out the head of the arrow," complained the soldier.

"That's an internal matter. That's a physician's business, not mine," was the reply.

任 事

又有医者,自称善外科,一裨将阵回①,中流矢,深入膜内,延使治。乃持并州剪②,剪去矢管,跪而请谢。

裨将曰:"镞在膜内者须亟治③。"

医曰:"此内科事,不意并责我!"

---

① 裨(pí皮)将:副将。裨,辅助、偏、小。
② 并州:古州名,在今山西省太原市一带地方,产剪刀有名。
③ 镞(cù促):箭头。

Laugh with Others

A blind man was in the company of others. When his companions saw something funny, they laughed. The blind man laughed, too.

When they asked him why he was laughing, the blind man replied, "Since you laugh, there must be something worth laughing at. Can you be cheating me there?"

众笑亦笑

一瞽者与众人坐①,众有所见而笑,瞽者亦笑。

众问之曰:"何所见而笑?"

瞽者曰:"你们所笑,定然不差②!"

---

① 瞽(gǔ 古):瞎子。
② 差:错误。

Fine Tung Wood

Gong Zhiqiao got some fine wood from a tung tree from which he fashioned a lute. When played, it made a very beautiful sound, the best in the world Gong thought. He presented it to the official in charge of rituals, who asked the court musicians to examine it. They said, "It's not a precious ancient one." So it was returned to Gong. At home he invited artists to paint it so that the texture looked old, and seal carvers to carve ancient inscriptions on it. Then he placed it in a box and buried it. One year later he went to sell it on the market. A nobleman bought it for a hundred taels of gold and presented it to the court. All the court musicians praised it, saying, "What a rare musical instrument!" When Gong heard about this, he sighed, "It's sad to realize that this is the way things are. This happens not only with this musical instrument, but also with everything else. I'd better go away or I'll land in trouble." So he fled deep into the mountains and disappeared.

良 桐

工之侨得良桐焉，斫而为琴，弦而鼓之，金声而玉应，自以为天下之美也，献之太常。使国工视之，曰："弗古。"还之。工之侨以归，谋诸漆工，作断纹焉；又谋诸篆工，作古窾焉；匣而埋诸土，期年出之，抱以适市。贵人过而见之，易之以百金。献诸朝，乐官传视，皆曰："希世之珍也。"工之侨闻之叹曰："悲哉世也！岂独一琴哉，莫不然矣。而不早图之，其与亡矣！"遂去，入于宕冥之山，不知其所终。

英汉对照
English-Chinese
中国文学宝库
Gems of Chinese Literature
古代文学系列
Classical Literature

Drought Assails the East Capital

At the end of the reign of Emperor Min Di in the Han Dynasty a long spell of drought assailed the east capital, so that even the grass was scorched and the lake dry.

A local sorcerer suggested to an elder of the district, "We'd better ask help from the divine creature in the south mountain." The elder answered, "That's no good. We know it's a flood dragon who'll bring us rain as well as future troubles." But the people said, "The drought is so serious that we feel we're sitting on stoves. We're unable to live today, so what's the use of worrying about tomorrow?" Therefore the people and the sorcerer went to the south mountain to pray for the monster to appear. Before their third libation was offered they saw the flood dragon wriggling out from a deep mountain pool and instantly a fierce wind blew down the mountain valley. Immediately there was a thunderstorm which lasted for more than three days. All the rivers flooded and the east capital was inundated. Then the people regretted not having listened to the advice of the elder.

东都大旱

汉愍帝之季年①,东都②大旱,野草皆焦,昆明之池③竭。洛巫④谓其父老曰:"南山之湫⑤,有灵物可起也。"父老曰:"是蛟⑥也,弗可用也,虽得雨,必有后忧。"众曰:"今旱极矣,人如坐炉炭,朝不谋夕,其暇计⑦后忧乎?"

乃召洛巫与如⑧湫,祷而起之。酒未毕三奠,蛟蜿蜒出,有风随之,飗飗然山谷皆殷⑨。有顷⑩,雷雨大至,木尽拔,弥⑪三日不止。伊洛瀍涧⑫皆溢,东都大困,始悔不用其父老之言。

① 愍(mín 民)。季年:末年。
② 东都:因西汉建都长安,故把河南洛阳称东都。
③ 昆明之池:汉武帝时曾在长安近郊挖地成池,周围四十里,名为昆明池。
④ 洛巫:洛水的巫婆。
⑤ 湫(qiū 秋):水潭。
⑥ 蛟:古代传说中的神物,能发洪水。
⑦ 其暇计:哪里有功夫考虑。其,岂,哪里。暇,闲空儿,功夫。计,考虑。
⑧ 如:往,到。
⑨ 殷(yīn 阴):震动。
⑩ 有顷:一会功夫。
⑪ 弥:满,整整。
⑫ 伊洛瀍涧:伊河、洛河、瀍(chán 缠)河、涧水。

英汉对照
English-Chinese
中国文学宝库
Gems of Chinese Literature
古代文学系列
Classical Literature

Saving a Tiger

Around the verdant mountain several streams merged into a river. A priest built a temple on the mountain and worshipped Buddha there. One night the water rose and debris from many dilapidated huts and houses floated in the flood. Victims on trunks and logs cried for help. The priest put on his straw rain cape and rowed a large boat on the water with some strong swimmers and ropes to save the people. When they saw a man in the water, they would throw him the rope. At daybreak, After having saved many lives, the priest saw an animal floating with its head above water. It glanced right and left as if begging for help. The priest told the boatmen, "It's also a living creature, we ought to hurry and save it." The boatmen threw logs into the water and helped it on board. The beast was a tiger. Gradually it recovered from its exhaustion and licked its fur. When they reached dry land the tiger glared hungrily at the priest and sprang on him. The boatmen hurried to his rescue, and fortunately the priest escaped with his life, though he was badly mauled.

道士救虎

苍筤之山①溪水合流入于江。有道士筑于其上以事佛②,甚谨③。

一夕,山水大出,漂室庐④,塞溪⑤而下。人骑木乘屋,号呼求救者声相连也。道士具⑥大舟,躬⑦蓑笠,立水浒⑧,督善水者绳⑨以俟。人至,即投木索引之,所存活甚众。

平旦⑩,有兽身没波涛中,而浮其首,左右盼,若求救者。道士曰:"是亦有生,必速救之。"舟者应言往,以木接上之,乃虎也。始则矇矇然⑪,坐而舐其毛;比及岸,则瞠目眂⑫道士。跃而攫之,仆地。舟人奔救,道士得不死,而重伤焉。

① 苍筤(láng 狼)之山:青山。
② 事佛:供奉神佛。
③ 甚谨:很恭谨、虔诚。
④ 庐:房屋。
⑤ 塞溪:充满了溪水。
⑥ 具:预备了。
⑦ 躬:身上。
⑧ 水浒:水边。
⑨ 绳:作动词用,拿着绳子。
⑩ 平旦:天亮的时候。
⑪ 矇矇然:神志不清,迷迷糊糊的样子。
⑫ 瞠(chēng 称)目眂(shì 是):瞪着眼睛看着。

英汉对照
English-Chinese
中国文学宝库
Gems of Chinese Literature
古代文学系列
Classical Literature

The Malicious Intent of Ziqiao

Xiguo Ziqiao, Gongsun Guisui and She Xu used to go out philandering, climbing over their neighbour's wall at night. The neighbours resented this and dug a manure pit in their path. One night the trio went out again. Ziqiao was the first to fall into the pit, but he urged Guisui to come too. As soon as Guisui fell into the pit, Ziqiao stopped him from warning Xu. Then Xu landed in the pit also. Ziqiao then said, "I didn't want you laughing at me, so I thought it better you fall in the muck too." A gentleman commented that Xiguo Ziqiao was not an honourable man. He had tarnished his reputation, but more than that, with malicious intent he even laid a trap for his friends. A men without any virtue!

西郭子侨

西郭子侨①与公孙诡随②、涉虚俱为微行③,昏夜逾其邻人之垣④,邻人恶之,坎⑤其往来之途而置溷焉。一夕又往,子侨先堕于溷,弗言,而招诡随,诡随从之堕,欲呼,子侨掩其口曰:"勿言。"俄而⑥涉虚至,亦堕。子侨乃言曰:"我欲其无相⑦哑⑧也。"

君子谓⑨西郭子侨非人也:己则不慎,自取污辱而包藏祸心⑩,以陷其友,其不仁⑪甚矣!

---

① 西郭子侨:虚拟的人名,复姓西郭。
② 公孙诡随:虚拟的人名,复姓公孙。
③ 微行:隐藏自己身份改装出行。
④ 垣(yuán 原):矮墙。
⑤ 坎:挖个坑。
⑥ 俄而:一会儿。
⑦ 无相:不(笑话)我。相,不是互相的意思,只涉及动作的一方。
⑧ 哑(xì 戏):大笑的样子。
⑨ 谓:认为。
⑩ 包藏祸心:心里藏着坏主意。
⑪ 不仁:不道德。

英汉对照
English-Chinese
中国文学宝库
Gems of Chinese Literature
古代文学系列
Classical Literature

The Musk Deer and the Tiger

A tiger chased a musk deer, which fled towards a precipice, crying and leaping over the cliff. The tiger followed. Both died. Yu Li Zi commented, "The musk deer had to jump, because it had no way out with the cliff ahead and the tiger behind. If the deer went back, it was doomed. If it leapt over the cliff, there was a slight chance of survival, and that was preferable to being devoured by the tiger. As for tiger, it could go forward or stop as it wished. So why did it choose to jump and die together with the musk deer? If the deer had not leapt, the tiger would not have met its end. That showed the tiger's stupidity and the deer's cleverness. Alas! Those who are avaricious and despotic like tigers ought to learn some lessons from this."

麋 虎

虎逐麋,麋奔而阚于崖,跃焉,虎亦跃而从之,俱坠而死。郁离子曰:"麋之跃于崖也,不得已也。前有崖而后有虎,进退死也。故退而得虎,则有死而无生之冀;进而跃焉,虽必坠,万一有无望之生,亦愈于坐而食于虎者也。若虎则进与退皆在我,无不得已也,而随以俱坠,何哉?麋虽死而与虎俱亡,使不跃于崖,则不能致虎之俱亡也。虽虎之冥亦麋之计得哉。呜呼,若虎可以为贪而暴者之永鉴矣!"

英汉对照
English-Chinese
中国文学宝库
Gems of Chinese Literature
古代文学系列
Classical Literature

Wisdom and Strength

Yu Li Zi said, "Compared to humans, the tiger's strength is more than double. With its sharp fangs and claws the tiger further increases its strength, so it is natural to have men eaten by tigers. However one does not often see people eaten by tigers, but the tiger's skin is commonly used by men as carpets. Why? The tiger relies on its strength, but man uses his wisdom. The tiger can only use its fangs and claws, but man can use other things; so the tiger's strength is equivalent to one, while man with his wisdom has a hundred times its strength. One, however powerful, against a hundred, cannot be always successful. A man is eaten by a tiger only if he is unable to use his wisdom and weapons. That is why it is said that he who only uses strength and not wisdom, or depends only on himself and not others, is like a tiger. It is no wonder such people are caught by others and their skins used as carpets."

智 力

郁离子曰："虎之力,于人不啻倍也。虎利其爪牙而人无之,又倍其力焉,则人之食于虎也无怪矣。然虎之食人不恒见,而虎之皮人常寝处之,何哉?虎用力,人用智,虎自用其爪牙,而人用物。故力之用一,而智之用百。爪牙之用各一,而物之用百,以一敌百,虽猛不必胜。故人之为虎食者,有智与物而不能用者也。是故天下之用力而不用智,与自用而不用人者,皆虎之类也,其为人独而寝处其皮也,何足怪哉?"

英汉对照
English-Chinese
中国文学宝库
Gems of Chinese Literature
古代文学系列
Classical Literature

Beekeepers

In Lingqiu an old man, good at apiculture, collected several hundred bushels of honey and wax respectively each year. His accumulated wealth equalled that of any lord. After his death his son took over. Less than a month later a swarm of bees flew away, but the son did not care. One year later half the bees moved away and the other half also left the following year. After that the son lived in poverty. When Fan Li, the well-known merchant, came to the district he asked about this. "Why has there been this change from past prosperity to present poverty?" An aged neighbour of the beekeeper answered, "It's because of the bees." Fan Li asked for details. The old man said, "In the past the father kept the bees meticulously. There was a house in the garden for some of his helpers. They hollowed out tree trunks and made them into solid hives which were positioned in an orderly fashion in suitable places. Five hives formed a group with a special person in charge of them. According to the rules of beekeeping, the temperature of the hives was appropriately adjusted and the hives always repaired. When the bees reproduced themselves too quickly, some were separated; when too slowly, their numbers were increased. They also kept only one queen bee. They were protected from ants,

灵丘丈人养蜂

灵丘①之丈人,善养蜂,岁收蜜数百斛②,蜡称之③,于是其富比封君④焉。丈人卒,其子继之,未期月,蜂有举族⑤去者,弗恤⑥也。岁余去且半,又岁余尽去,其家遂贫。

陶朱公⑦之齐,过而问焉,曰:"是何昔者之,熇熇⑧,而今日之凉凉⑨也?"其邻之叟对曰:"以蜂。"请问其故,对曰:"昔者丈人之养蜂也,园有庐,庐有守,刳木⑩以为蜂之宫,不罅不疈⑪。其置也,疏密有行,新旧有次,坐有方⑫,牖有向。五五为伍,一人司之。视其生息,调其喧寒,巩其构架,时其墐发⑬。蕃⑭则

---

① 灵丘:地名,山东滕县东。
② 斛(hú 户):古代十斗为一斛。
③ 称之:和蜜相等。称,适合,相等。
④ 封君:受有封地的人。
⑤ 举族:整窝,整箱。举,全。
⑥ 恤(xù 胥):忧虑。
⑦ 陶朱公:即春秋时期的范蠡,助越灭吴后去经商,改名为陶朱公。
⑧ 熇熇(hè 贺):火势旺盛的样子。
⑨ 凉凉:自甘寂寞,引申为凄凉。
⑩ 刳(kū 枯):挖空木头。
⑪ 不疈(yǒu 有):(蜂房)不朽坏。
⑫ 坐有方:坐置有方向。
⑬ 墐(yìn 进)发:用泥涂塞。
⑭ 蕃:繁殖。从,同纵,放走。析,分开。

英汉对照
English-Chinese
中国文学宝库
Gems of Chinese Literature
古代文学系列
Classical Literature

spiders, pests, flies and wasps, from scorching sun in summer and freezing cold in winter, from strong winds and heavy rain. The amount of honey taken from the bees was limited only to what was in excess, instead of exhausting their supply at one go. Therefore the old bees remained and the new ones reproduced, and that was why the father got rich staying at home. But his son was different. He did not repair the garden and the house, clear away rubbish or keep the hives dry and cool, but opened and shut them at will. The hives became very uncomfortable and it was difficult for the bees to fly in and out. Of course the bees weren't happy about this. Then caterpillars moved in with the bees, and ants invaded the honeycombs. Birds caught them in daytime and foxes at night. But the son was only interested in collecting honey and paid no attention to their miserable state. Naturally the bees went away." Fan Li commented, "Yes, you must take note of this, and those who govern the country and people should draw some lessons from it."

灵丘丈人养蜂

从之,析之,寡则与之①,裒之,不使有二王也。去其蛦蟊、蚍蜉②,弥③其土蜂、蝇豹。夏不烈日,冬不凝澌,飘风吹而不摇,淋雨沃而不渍④,其取蜜也,分其赢而已矣,不竭其力也。于是故者安⑤,新者息,丈人不出户而收其利。今其子则不然矣,园庐不葺,污秽不治,燥湿不调,启闭无节,居处龃龉⑥,出入障碍,而蜂不乐其居矣。及其久也,蛅蟖⑦同其房而不知,蝼蚁钻其室而不禁,鹩鹆⑧掠之于白日,狐狸窃之于昏夜,莫之察也。取蜜而已,又焉得不凉凉也哉!"

陶朱公曰:"噫⑨,二三子识之:为国⑩有民者,可以鉴矣。"

① 与之:帮助它们。裒(póu),聚集起来。
② 蛦蟊、蚍蜉(cǎi 采 máo 毛、pí 皮 fú 伏):斑蟊和大蚂蚁。
③ 弥(mí 迷):消除。蝇豹,蜘蛛。
④ 不渍(zì 自):不受浸泡。
⑤ 故者安:先养的蜜蜂安心。
⑥ 龃龉(niè wù 聂务):动摇不安。
⑦ 蛅蟖(zhān sī 沾司):毛毛虫。
⑧ 鹩鹆(liáo yù 辽玉):鹩鹆和寒鸦。
⑨ 噫:唉。
⑩ 为国:治理国家。

英汉对照
English-Chinese
中国文学宝库
Gems of Chinese Literature
古代文学系列
Classical Literature

A Merchant

The boat of a merchant from Jiyin sank while it was crossing a river. The merchant perched on some floating flotsam, crying for help. A fishermen rowed his boat to the rescue. Spotting his helper the merchant anxiously shouted, "I come from a wealthy family in Jiyin. I'll pay a hundred taels to the man who saves my life!" The fisherman then helped him ashore, but the merchant only gave him ten taels instead of a hundred. The fisherman complained, "You promised a hundred taels but you've only given me ten." The merchant answered angrily, "A fisherman like you earns very little each day. Now you get ten taels and you're complaining?" The fisherman left in dejection. Later the merchant travelled from Lüliang on a boat which was wrecked on some rocks. It happened that the same fisherman was present and someone asked him, "Should we save him?" The fisherman answered, "He is the one who broke his promise." So all the fishermen kept away and the merchant was drowned.

济阴商人

济阴①之贾人,渡河而亡其舟,栖于浮苴②之上,号焉。有渔者以舟往救之,未至,贾人急号曰:"我济上之巨室③也,能捄④我,予尔百金。"渔者载而升诸陆,则予十金,渔者曰:"向许⑤百金,而今予十金,无乃⑥不可乎?!"贾人勃然作色曰:"若渔者也,一日之获几何!而骤得十金,犹为不足乎?"渔者黯然⑦而退。

他日,贾人浮⑧吕梁而下,舟薄⑨于石又覆,而渔者在焉。人曰:"盍救诸⑩?"渔者曰:"是⑪许金而不酬者也。"立而观之,遂没。

---

① 济阴:地名,在济水之南,今山东荷泽附近。贾人,商人。
② 浮苴(chá苴):漂着的枯草。
③ 巨室:世家大族。济上,济水边上。
④ 捄(jū苴):以手揪拔。
⑤ 向许:刚才答应。
⑥ 无乃:莫非,岂不是。
⑦ 黯然:沮丧的样子。
⑧ 浮:乘船。吕梁,古代的河名。下,顺流而下。
⑨ 薄:靠近,这里是碰撞的意思。覆,翻了船。
⑩ 盍(hé合)救诸:为什么不救他呢。盍,何不。诸,之乎的合音。
⑪ 是:这(个人)。不酬,不给。

英汉对照
English-Chinese
中国文学宝库
Gems of Chinese Literature
古代文学系列
Classical Literature

The Nine-Headed Bird

On Boyao Mountain there was a bird with nine heads. Whenever one of the heads snatched at food, all the other eight contended for it. They fought and pecked each other, their blood oozing and their feathers flying. Finally all nine heads were injured and could not eat any food. A sea bird watching the scene laughed. "Why don't you think that the food which enters your nine mouths fills the same belly? There's no reason for you nine heads to vie with each other."

九头鸟争食

擘摇之虚①有鸟焉,一身而九头,得食则八头皆争,呀然②而相衔③,洒血飞毛,食不得入咽,而九头皆伤。海凫④观而笑之曰:"而⑤胡不思,九口之食,同归于一腹乎?而奚⑥其争也。"

---

① 擘(bò 簸)摇之虚:神话传说中的山名,虚同墟,山。
② 呀然:张着嘴。然,样子。
③ 相衔:互相争食。
④ 海凫(fú 富):一种海鸟。
⑤ 而:同尔,你。胡,何,为什么。
⑥ 奚:何,为什么。

英汉对照
English-Chinese
中国文学宝库
Gems of Chinese Literature
古代文学系列
Classical Literature

Jue Shu's Three Regrets

Jue Shu was self-confident and liked to oppose others' advice. Once, while farming in Guiyin, he tried to grow rice on the plain and millet in the swamp. His friend told him, "Millet likes dry, high land and rice a swamp. You grow them the other way round and contrary to nature. How will you get any harvest from them?" Jue Shu ignored his friend's advice. After ten years his granary was still empty. When he went to his friend's fields and saw his harvested crops, he bowed to his friend, saying, "To my regret I now know my mistake." Later on he embarked on a business venture at Wenshang market. Scrambling for the goods in great demand, he always competed with the other merchants. When he bought some commodities, the other merchants did likewise and the market was flooded with them. So Jue Shu always failed in business. His friend told him, "A wise and clever merchant buys what is not in great demand and waits for an opportunity to make a good profit. That is how Bai

蹶叔三悔

蹶叔① 好自信,而喜违人言②,田③ 于龟阴,取其原④ 为稻而隰⑤ 为粱。其友谓之曰:"粱喜亢⑥,稻喜隰,而子反之,失其性⑦ 矣,其何以能获?"弗听,积十稔⑧,而仓无储,乃视其友之田,莫不如所言以获,乃拜⑨ 曰:"予知悔矣。"

既而商于汶上⑩,必相⑪ 货之急于时者趋之⑫,无所往而不与人争,比⑬ 得,而趋者毕至,辄⑭ 不获市。其友又谓之曰:"善贾者,收人所不争,时来⑮ 利必倍,此白圭⑯ 之所以

---

① 蹶(jué 决)叔:虚拟的人名。
② 违人言:不听从别人的话。
③ 田:作动词用,种田。龟阴,虚拟的地名。
④ 原:高地。
⑤ 隰(xí 席):低洼湿地。
⑥ 亢:高。反之,做法相反。
⑦ 性:本性,规律。
⑧ 稔(rěn 忍):庄稼成熟。
⑨ 拜:作揖。
⑩ 汶上:地名,在山东。商,经商。
⑪ 相:观察。急于时者,当时急需的货物。
⑫ 趋之:奔向那里。
⑬ 比:等到。
⑭ 辄(zhé 哲):往往。市,动词,卖出去。
⑮ 时来:时机一到。
⑯ 白圭:战国时工商奴隶主,使用奴隶经商,投机致富。

英汉对照
English-Chinese
中国文学宝库
Gems of Chinese Literature
古代文学系列
Classical Literature

Jue Shu's Three Regrets

Gui, the well-known merchant, became successful." Jue Shu ignored his friend's advice. After ten years he was in great straits. Recalling his friend's suggestion, he bowed to him, saying, "Now I know my mistake, and I am full of regrets again." Later he planned a sea voyage, and asked his friend to accompany him. They drifted eastward and came to a big gulf. His friend told him, "Over there is Gui Xu, a bottomless gulf. If you go there, you'll never come back." Jue Shu ignored his friend's advice and continued his journey and got trapped in the gulf. After nine years with the help of enormous waves he was fortunately driven ashore. When he reached home he was haggerd, his hair grey, and hardly recognizable. He paid a visit to his friend, bowing with gratitude, and then swore by heaven, "I swear by the sun never to do it again." His friend smiled, saying, "You've felt remorse three times, what's the use of worrying any more?"

Someone commented that Jue Shu should not have regretted anything and be carefree, rather than feel remorse thrice till he grew old.

富也。"弗听,又十年而大困①,复思其言而拜曰:"予今而后,不敢不悔矣。"

他日以舶入于海,要② 其友与偕,则泛滥③ 而东,临于巨渊,其友曰:"是归塘④ 也,往且不可复⑤。又弗听,则入于大壑⑥ 之中,九年得化鲲之涛⑦嘘之以还。比还而发尽白,形如枯腊⑧,人无识之者。乃再拜⑨稽首以谢其友,仰天而矢⑩ 之曰:"予所弗悔者有如日。"其友笑曰:"悔则悔矣,夫何及乎?"

人谓蹶叔三悔以没齿⑪,不如不悔之无忧也。

---

① 大困:遇到大的困难。复,又。
② 要:同邀,请。与偕,和他一块儿去。
③ 泛滥:浮沉,在水中漂流。巨渊,深海。
④ 归塘:也称归墟,在渤海之东的深海,无底。
⑤ 复:回来。
⑥ 大壑:深的海沟。
⑦ 化鲲(kūn 坤)之涛:巨大的波涛。嘘之,吹他。
⑧ 枯腊(xī 西):干肉。
⑨ 再拜:两次叩头,行最大的礼。稽首,叩头礼拜。
⑩ 矢:同誓,发誓。
⑪ 没齿:一辈子。

英汉对照
English-Chinese
中国文学宝库
Gems of Chinese Literature
古代文学系列
Classical Literature

An Impetuous Person

An impetuous person lived somewhere between the Kingdom of Jin and the Kingdom of Zhen during the Warring States Period. If he missed the target while shooting, he smashed it. If he lost a chess game, he gnawed the pieces. Somenone told him, "It's not the fault of the target or the chess pieces. What about blaming yourself?" He did not pay attention to this, and finally died of anger.

躁 人

昔郑之间① 有躁人② 焉,射不中则碎其鹄③,奕④不胜则啮其子⑤,人曰:是非⑥鹄与子之罪也,盍⑦ 亦反而思之乎?"弗喻⑧,卒⑨病躁而死。

---

① 郑之间:郑国国内。
② 躁人:性情急躁的人。
③ 鹄(gǔ 古):靶子。
④ 奕:下棋。
⑤ 啮(niè)其子:咬那棋子。
⑥ 是非:这不是。
⑦ 盍:何不。
⑧ 弗喻:不明白道理。
⑨ 卒:终于。病,困,苦。

英汉对照
English-Chinese
中国文学宝库
Gems of Chinese Literature
古代文学系列
Classical Literature

Stealing Dregs

A man liked to argue with others over the Buddhist scriptures and show off his interpretations in a smug manner. Yu Li Zi told him, "In the land of Lu, people could not make good wine, but the people in Zhongshan could, so the people of Lu tried to get the secret but failed. Someone who held an official post in Zhongshan once stayed in a wine shop and stole some of the dregs. He soaked the dregs in local wine and presented it to others, saying, 'This is the wine of Zhongshan.' Those who drank it thought it was the real stuff. One day the proprietor of the wine shop arrived. When he heard there was wine, he asked for some. After tasting it, he spat it out and said with a smile, 'It's made of the dregs from my wine.' Now, you can parade your Buddhist scriptures before me, but I wonder if a real Buddhist might laugh at the dregs you've stolen."

鲁人窃糟

客有好佛者①,每与人论道理,必以其说驾之②,欣欣然自以为有独得③焉。郁离子谓之曰:"昔者④,鲁人⑤不能为酒,惟中山之人⑥善酿千日之酒。鲁人求其方⑦,弗得。有仕⑧于中山者,主⑨酒家,取其糟⑩归,以鲁酒渍之⑪,谓人曰:'中山之酒也'。鲁人饮之,皆以为中山之酒也。一日,酒家之主者⑫来,闻有酒,索⑬而饮之,吐而笑曰:'是予之糟液也'。今子以佛夸予可也,吾恐真佛之笑子窃其'糟'也。"

---

① 好佛者:信奉佛教的人。
② 驾之:超越过别人。
③ 独得:独到的见解。欣欣然,高兴的样子。
④ 昔者:从前。
⑤ 鲁人:鲁国人。
⑥ 中山之人:中山国的人。
⑦ 方:配方。
⑧ 仕:做官。
⑨ 主:主持,掌管。
⑩ 糟:酒糟。
⑪ 渍(zì 自)之:浸泡它。
⑫ 主者:主人。
⑬ 索:求要。

英汉对照
English-Chinese
中国文学宝库
Gems of Chinese Literature
古代文学系列
Classical Literature

Preemptive Surgery

On hearing the views of a man afar that asserted the liver of a horse to be highly toxic and capable of poisoning people, Emperor Wu of the Han Dynasty once said: "Wen Cheng died after eating a horse's liver." These words caused great amusement to Yu Gong who observed: "This is ridiculous! While in the body of the horse it does not cause the horse to die, does it?" The stranger retorted in jest: "Well, I've never seen a horse that could reach the advanced age of a man, say one hundred, have you? This is due to its liver."

Yu Gong was suddenly won over. Since he had a horse himself, he went out and removed its liver and the horse died instantly. He then cast down his knife and remarked with a sigh: "Indeed, it must have been poisonous, since the horse could not live long after its removal. Obviously it would have been even worse if the thing had been allowed to remain inside the body of the horse!"

刳马肝

有客语马肝大毒,能杀人,故汉武帝云:"文成食马肝而死。"迂公适闻之,发笑曰:"客诳语耳,肝故在马腹中,马何以不死?"客戏曰:"马无百年之寿,以有肝故也。"公大悟,家有畜马,便刳其肝,马立毙。公掷刀叹曰:"信哉,毒也。去之尚不可活,况留肝乎?"

A Bull Wearing a Kerchief

When a rich man ordered his cowherd to dry a kerchief in the sun, the cowherd put it on the horns of a bull. While drinking at a stream the bull was startled by its reflection in the water and stamped off into the distance, leaving the cowherd to trail behind, and forcing him all along the way to ask people: "Have you seen a bull wearing a kerchief?"

富翁戴巾

财主命牧童晒巾,童晒之牛角上。牛临水照视,惊而走逸。童问人曰:"见一只戴巾牛否?"

Better to Be Blind

As they were walking together, two blind men mused: "The blind are truly the most fortunate people in the world. Those with good eyes have to spend their days slaving away, particulary all those peasants! They will never know the splendid luxury of our leisure!" But their words were overheard by some farmers who, pretending to be officials, shouted at them to make way and, because they were unable to do so in time, ordered that they should be beaten with a hoe handle. They were then ordered to make haste in leaving the place. As they did so, however, one of them was overheard to say: "It is still better to be blind. People with sight after they get beaten would be sentenced as well!"

宁为盲人

二聋者同行,曰:"世上惟聋者最好,有眼人终日奔忙,农家更甚,怎得如我们清闲一世。"适众农夫窃听之,乃假为官人,谓其失于回避,以锄榔各打一顿,而呵之去,随后复窃听之,一聋者曰:"毕竟是聋者好,若是有眼人,打了还要问罪。"

英汉对照
English-Chinese
中国文学宝库
Gems of Chinese Literature
古代文学系列
Classical Literature

Parents for Sale

A foolish son was looking after his father's store when the old man was out on business. A man appeared and asked: "Do you have *zunweng* (an honorific term for someone's father) here?" The reply was: "No!" The man again asked: "Is *zuntang* (a polite reference to another's mother) here?" The reply was also "No!"

The father, on learning what had come to pass during his absence, said: "Look, by *zunweng* he meant your father and *zuntang* refers to your mother."

The son seemed vexed and after some time exclaimed: "How was I to know the both of you were for sale?"

卖双亲

有呆子者,父出门,令其守店。忽有买货者至,问:"尊翁有么?"曰:"无。""尊堂有么?"亦曰:"无。"父归知之,谓子曰:"尊翁,我也;尊堂,汝母也,何得言无?"子懊怒曰:"谁知你夫妇两人都是要卖的。"

Evading a Debt

A debtor not only refused to make good on his word, but further deceived his creditor, saying: "At present I am courting a rich widow. The only thing is that I do not have enough money for a betrothal gift. If you could find it in your heart to help me out, I shall have enough money not only to repay you but to lend to you in the future!"

Believing his words, the creditor extended him further loans. Once he had the money, the debtor used a portion of it to repair and redecorate his house, causing the creditor to think it a more plausible story.

One day the creditor was passing before his gate and decided to knock at the door. Inside, he heard a woman's voice call toward the door: "My husband is out presently." This same response was repeated on several other occasions. Growing suspicious, the creditor finally peeped through a hole in one of the paper windows. There he saw no woman at all in the room, only the debtor standing there himself impersonating a woman's voice and pinching his nose with his fingers.

The enraged creditor broke in through the window and a flurry of blows descended upon the man, who just stood there taking it, with his nose still pinched and yelling: "If my husband owes you, what has that to do with me!"

躲 债

欠债不应所索,反诳之曰:"我有头亲事,是寡妇,饶有私蓄,只可惜无本钱下礼,汝若助我取来,不但可还前欠,还有得借你。"其人信以为实,出银帮之。此人得银,先将房屋装折齐整,其人愈信。他日过其门而叩之,闻内有妇人声应曰:"拙夫出外去了。"如是数过,不觉心动,因穴窗窥之,见无妇人,乃此人捻鼻所为,大怒,破窗而入,乱拳殴之,其人犹捻鼻喊云:"拙夫欠债,却与奴家何干。"

可谓久假而不归矣。

英汉对照
English-Chinese
中国文学宝库
Gems of Chinese Literature
古代文学系列
Classical Literature

Retractility

One day a father lectured his son, saying: "Retractility is an important element in rhetorical style; cut and dry statements, on the other hand, are a pitfall." But the son interrupted and asked: "What do you mean by 'retractility'?"

At this juncture, a neighbor came in with a request to borrow some household articles from them. The father told his son: "Now see here, if someone wants to borrow some items, you should say neither that you have everything nor that you have nothing. Merely reply that some are available to lend and some not. This is the essence of retractility in speech. It applies to many other human affairs as well." The son made sure to take his father's words to heart.

On another day, when a visitor came and inquired: "Is your honorable father in?" The son replied: "To a certain extent, yes; to a certain extent, no…"

答令尊

　　父教子曰:"凡人说话放活脱些,不可一句说煞。"子问:"如何叫做活脱?"此时适邻家有借几件器物的,父指谓曰:"假如这家来借物件,不可竟说多有,不可竟说多无,只说也有在家的,也有不在家的,这话就活脱了,凡事俱可类推。"子记之。他日有客到门,问:"令尊翁在家么?"子答曰:"也有在家的,也有不在家的。"

英汉对照
English-Chinese
中国文学宝库
Gems of Chinese Literature
古代文学系列
Classical Literature

To Readers of the English Translations of Classical Chinese Prose and Poetry

Chinese classical literature has a very long history. Some of the earliest works have left us questions that have baffled literary researchers for centuries. It has been difficult to find out the authors of some works, to interpret particular phrases and sentences, or to confirm the reliability of various versions of certain works. This gives rise to some questions in reading these translations. Here are some explanatory remarks.

Perhaps the earliest fables are taken from arguments of rhetoricians of the Spring and Autumn and Warring State periods, a tumultuous age when different schools of thoughts contended heatedly. Their debates and arguments were recorded in different books. Those rhetoricians were good at inventing witty parables, sometimes using animals as heroes, to support their opinions about certain events or people. Some fables were too closely bound with their contexts without which their morals might seem obscure (— if you find it hard to get the points of some fables, please remember this.) They were originally part of speeches and therefore had no definite titles. Some of the titles added later to them have been well accepted and even have become idioms in everyday Chinese, while others are just improvisations.

Similarly, the titles of some prose works were added by later editors or publishers. Some early books have been lost and today we can only see fragments of them in literary collections and anthologies. Often, different collections have different versions of the same pieces. That's why sometimes you see different titles for the same works or find details missing from or added to some stories.

The titles for the so-called *ci* poems are very peculiar. To understand them one must know the origin of that genre. "*Ci*" literally meaning "words" were words of songs. They were sung to music. Early *ci* were created by non-literati musicians active at the grassroots level. Their songs were much livelier and freer than scholars' creation, conveying ordinary people's aspirations and feelings. But since there are fewer musicians than poets, people tend to adapt the same melodies to new words. Just as we sing to the same tune the words: "In the canyon, in the... oh my darling Clementine..." and "Happy new year, happy new year, happy new year to you all..."; or, "Twinkle, twinkle little star..." and "A B C D E F G...". Later on literati writers took up this form of poetry. But since not many writers could compose music, they simply imitated the forms of existing songs and thus their works consisted of verses of different lengths. The "words" were finally divorced from the music (there have been, of course, exceptions — few *ci* poets, such as Jiang Kui, were good musicians and they created new forms). Unfortunately, in translation the forms of *ci* disappear. The reader of English translations usually cannot see much difference between the *ci* and other forms of classical Chinese poetry. Originally each song had a title reflecting its contents. When the same melody was adapted to new words, the title remained. By and by the title became irrelevant to the contents. Writers used the title as an indication of the pattern of forms used. Still later when the music was lost, *ci* simply became names of verse forms. Most *ci* writers entitled their works only by the names of the melodies and, occasionally, they give their works subtitles that reflect the contents. Different translators handle the titles in different ways. Some translators have tried to render the meaning of the titles in English. But since today the meanings of those titles are irrelevant to the contents of the *ci* poems, the semantic interpretation of the titles may sound queer and be meaningless. For the *ci* poems which have only the melody names as their titles some translators have given new titles indicative of the meaning of the whole piece (which may be helpful to English-speaking readers). To give a uniform appearance to our series, we rearranged the titles of *ci* poems, using the names of melodies as the titles which are merely transliterations from Chinese. We have kept the original subtitles added by the authors but cut the titles added by translators.

The translations of these classical Chinese works have been done through several decades and by different hands. They are in different styles and in terms of quality, they are not necessarily equally satisfactory. Sometimes the ambiguity lies in the structure of the Chinese language. For example, in Li Qingzhao's poem to the tune of *Yong Yu Le*, the following line "人在何处" (where is the person) has different interpretations: 人 may be understood as "I" or someone else. One translator rendered this line as: "where has my love gone." According to another interpretation, this line may be translated as "where am I now." Since absolutely "accurate" translation is not always possible and different translators naturally have different interpretations, by and large we have left the translations as they first appeared. We have done a few changes only where we thought the original rendering might have been too misleading.

If there are any errors caused by our editing, we beg the pardon of our translators and readers.

Revisor

关于中国古典文学作品英译文的说明

这些作品的译文都是在《中国文学》杂志英文版上发表过的,不是完成于一时一人之手,译文风格各异,质量也不尽整齐。古书版本歧异,加之古代汉语与现代汉语差别很大,不同的人对某些字句也会有不同的理解(因此读者可能会发现某些译文与汉语原文注释不吻合)。此次分类结集出版,除极个别明显误译的字句外一般不作改动。中国古代寓言有很多取自先秦诸家言论集,大多是为论证某一论点而即兴编造的,有些寓言脱离原来的上下文后不易懂其要旨,某些寓言原文太简,有的译者在译文中加以适当的润饰,使现代读者读来更有趣味,凡是不背离原文原意的,就保留了原译者的译文。有些古代散文作品原书已佚,今天只能散见于各种文集中,不同文集所收同一作品字句常有出入,甚至题目也是后人加的,因此读者可能会发现同一文章的不同题目和不同文字。考虑到本丛书是一般欣赏和学习读物,我们未作版本方面的考证。吕叔湘说得好,译诗无直译意译之分,唯有平实与工巧之别。本丛书所收的诗歌译文,有的紧扣原文,有的发挥较多。读者见仁见智,可以自己去比较。词历来多以词牌名为题,其字面义每与词意了不相干(如一首"西江月"可能根本不写"江""月")。不同译者常有不同的处理方法,如有的译者根据词的内容另拟新题,有的译者则把原词牌名意译。此次出版一律以音译词牌名作为词的题目,有原作者所加题目的保留原题作为副题。这样处理是否合适,请读者指点,并请原译者鉴谅。

——校译者